DIAMOND DREAMS

BOOK ONE
STRONG SOUTHERN WOMEN SERIES

ALI SPOONER

DIAMOND DREAMS

BOOK ONE
STRONG SOUTHERN WOMEN SERIES

ALI SPOONER

Affinity
Rainbow Publications

2018

Diamond Dreams
© 2018 by Ali Spooner

Affinity E-Book Press NZ LTD
Canterbury, New Zealand

1st Edition

ISBN: 978-1-98-854915-6

Editor: JoSelle Vanderhooft
Proof Editor: Alexis Smith
Cover Design: Irish Dragon Designs

ACKNOWLEDGMENTS

I would like to thank my fans for following my stories, providing great feedback and encouragement. Writing wouldn't be so much fun without you. Thanks to Affinity Rainbow Publishing, Irish Dragon for the cover art and the team of editors, readers, and publishers who continue to help me grow as a writer. Thank you to Rhonda for being patient with me when I have the urge to write.

DEDICATION

To Gail and Deborah, thanks for always being there.

TABLE OF CONTENTS

ALSO BY ALI SPOONER

SINGLE STORIES
The Bee Charmer
Ruined
Back in the Saddle
Open Your Heart
South of Heaven
Shotgun Rider
The Settlement
Love's Playlist
Cowgirl Up
Twisted Lives
The Epitaph
Terminal Event
Bailey's Run

SERIES
The Island Series
Neptune's Ring
Venus Rising

The Hunter Series
Bound
The Devil's Tree

Sasha Thibodaux Series
Sugarland
Bayou Justice
Line of Sight

CHAPTER ONE

The ball made a loud pop as it whizzed past Cameron St. Angelo and hit the leather of the catcher's mitt. The inside pitch was meant to brush her back from the plate, but Cam barely twitched as the ball breezed right past her face. After the umpire bellowed, "Ball two," Cam stepped out of the batter's box and tapped the aluminum bat against the metal cleats on both shoes. She turned her head toward the pitcher's mound and grinned. "Is that the best you got, Bugsy?"

"You damn well know it isn't," the pitcher growled back.

"Are y'all gonna play ball or jabber the rest of the game?"

Cam stepped back into the batter's box. "Sorry, Blue." She twisted her right foot in the packed clay until she felt comfortable and dropped her hand, indicating she was ready for the next pitch.

"'Bout damn time, St. Angelo," the catcher barked. "This gear is hot, so let's get a move on."

"Bring it," she called out to the pitcher.

1

Ursula Bugg, or Bugsy to Cam, was a top-ranked pitcher on the opposing team, and Cam knew she had a wicked-fast rise ball. She also knew that Ursula had a weakness and it was Cam herself. They had competed against each other in every sport since they first met in high school, and Cam had always proven to be the superior athlete. As hard as she tried, Bugsy had never bested her in any sport, and facing Cam now as the opposing pitcher would make no difference. Yes, Bugsy was good, but Cam was better, and she understood how much she got into Bugsy's head. They'd battled through three years in high school, and by their senior year, Bugsy's frustration had grown to an obsession. Bugsy's continued attempts to flirt with her creeped her out at first, but Cam learned to deal with Bugsy by ignoring her comments and gently reminding Bugsy that she had no interest in dating her.

It didn't matter that Cam was an all-state shortstop and the team's leading cleanup hitter, bound for Baton Rouge in the fall with a full ride to play softball for LSU. Bugsy was determined to strike her out. Cam could almost hear the grinding of Bugsy's teeth as she reached deep down inside for extra strength and released the next pitch.

"High and wide," the umpire called out. "Three balls and one strike."

Forced to throw a strike, or risk walking her, Bugsy stepped off the mound to wipe her hand, as Cam waited on the fastball that would be nestled in the center of the plate. Bugsy then stepped up to the pitching rubber, using the toe of her right foot to dig the hole beside it deeper for more traction and power, then begin her windup. She moved as if in slow motion to Cam, and the ball looked the size of a cantaloupe as it approached. Cam's eyes locked on their target as she tucked her chin to her chest and started her swing. Her teammates were probably holding their breath,

2

but Cam had no doubts the ball was leaving the park. She caught the ball on the sweet spot of her bat, and it sailed out of the park for a walk-off home run. She rushed out of the batter's box toward first base as the left fielder backed toward the fence until she realized there was no keeping the ball in the field of play. Cam rounded the base and slowed her pace to a jog as Bugsy glared at her from the pitcher's mound. When her cleated foot touched home, the umpire called, "Ball game."

Welcomed by her teammates with high fives and slaps to her helmet, Cam made her way to the dugout to drop off her gear before joining her friends in congratulating the other team on a game well played. When she approached Bugsy at the end of the line, she smiled. "See you next fall."

"You better believe it," Bugsy answered, finally cracking a smile. She would also be attending LSU to play softball. "Maybe we'll meet again next week if we make it to the tournament."

†

As they packed their gear, Cam looked over and smiled at her childhood friend, Brenda Toussant. "Are you still coming over tonight, Bren? Dad's not cooking, so we can go over to the camp for a fire and maybe a few brews."

"Dontcha know it. I've been looking forward to the weekend. Just think, in three more weeks, we'll be high school graduates."

"Yes, we will. Have you given any more thought to college?"

"Thought, yes, but there's no way we can afford tuition, and going to another school just wouldn't be fun without you."

3

Cam's heart sank, but she knew Bren was right. The tuition at LSU was expensive, and Bren's parents were struggling to raise her five younger siblings. They both knew the eventuality of Bren's future was to miss out on college and go straight from high school to work, but for now, they would enjoy the last few weeks of freedom.

Cam draped her arm across Bren's shoulder as they carried their bags to the bus for the short ride back to school. On the way, the team sang along at the top of their lungs to Lynyrd Skynyrd.

"See ya when I see ya," Cam teased as she pulled Bren into a hug. "Be careful. I'll be ready by the time you come over."

"I'll be there as quick as I can. Daddy's going to let me use his truck, but I've got to be home before midnight."

"I wish you could stay, but I've got to be up early too. I promised to help Dad with cutting some sugarcane."

Bren disappeared into a crowd of sweaty boys as spring football practice ended and they headed to the showers. Cam's heart ached when Bren raised up on her tiptoes to plant a kiss on Rudy Merchant's lips. Rudy had graduated two years earlier, and had been hired as an assistant coach for the football team. Bren and Rudy had dated for the last four years, and Cam was almost certain he would ask Bren to marry him after she graduated. That's what everyone expected, and her moving out of the house would mean one fewer mouth for her daddy to feed. Rudy was a good guy and treated Bren kindly, even though she was making him wait until after they were married to have sex. The thought of Bren in another's arms made Cam shiver.

She turned away and strolled over to her Jeep. She was no beauty, but Cam and her dad had gotten her running, and so far, she had proven reliable. Cam had heard her parents talking about giving the Jeep a paint job for her graduation present. She grinned at herself in the rearview mirror. *Bren gets an engagement ring and I get a paint job. At least I'll have a few more years of freedom before I have to decide where my future lies.*

She pulled away from the curb and drove for home, the lyrics to "Sweet Home Alabama" still playing in her head. When she turned into the long drive leading to her house, her eight-year-old baby sister Sandy was searching the ditch for crawfish. Cam pulled the Jeep to a halt when Sandy rushed over to her.

"Hiya, Cam."

"What you doing, Squirt?"

"Looking for crawdads." She beamed.

"Find any?"

"Just a couple, but I let them go."

Cam smiled at her. "Hop in."

Sandy was barely tall enough to open the door, and Cam reached across and offered her a hand to climb into the Jeep. She saw Cam's uniform. "Did you win today?"

"Is it hot out?"

"It's a bit warm."

"Yes, we won, and your big sister hit a home run. How was your day at school?"

"It was good. I had a home run, too, in our kickball game."

"Awesome." Cam offered her a high five. "I have to help Dad with harvesting some sugarcane tomorrow, but when I get done, why don't we check some cages and see if we can round up enough mudbugs for dinner tomorrow night?"

"I'd like that, Cam."

"When we get home, I'll check with Mama and see if that's okay with her."

"Is Bren coming out tonight?"

Cam noticed the sparkle in her baby sister's eyes and wondered if she wasn't the only St. Angelo crushing on Bren. "Yes, she is. We're going over to the Island for a campfire at the hunt camp." Sandy drew in a deep breath. "No, before you ask, you can't go with us tonight."

"Aw, Cam. Why not? Are you two meeting boys over there or something?"

She couldn't hold back her chuckle. "Nope, no boys allowed, and no baby sisters either." Cam ruffled Sandy's hair. "Don't worry, we'll have all afternoon."

Sandy poked out her bottom lip in her best attempt at a pout. Cam ignored the plea. "Crank up that window for me, please."

With an audible huff, Sandy turned the metal crank to raise the passenger-side window.

"C'mon, let's go see what Mom's cooking. I don't know about you, but I could eat a horse." Cam walked around to the passenger side and took out her bag. "Hop on, Squirt," she said and turned her back to Sandy.

Sandy wrapped her legs around Cam's hips, and arms around her shoulders. "Giddyup, Horse."

Cam twisted to the right, then spun back to the left, but remained conscious of the precious cargo clinging to her neck. "Better hold on tight," she warned and bolted for the side door.

Her mother, Camille, and sister, Teresa, were in the kitchen preparing dinner when they raced through the door.

"Whoa, slow down, you two. You gonna make my cornbread fall with that commotion," their mama teased.

Cam spun one last time before lowering Sandy to her feet. "Will you carry my bag to my room?"

"Sure, Cam."

Sandy raced from the kitchen as Cam kissed her mama's cheek. "What you got smelling so good in here?"

"Swamp cabbage, fried fatback, cornbread, and Teresa's going to try her hand at creamed corn tonight."

"Ewwee, there's gonna be some gas up in this house tonight."

"When isn't there?" Camille replied.

Cam chuckled. "You do have a point there, Mama. Are you up for a boil tomorrow night? I promised Sandy I'd take her out to check some crawfish traps tomorrow, if you were up to having a boil."

"That does sound good," T chimed in. "Would you mind if I invited Buster out?"

"Good Lord, I'll have to find a lot of mudbugs if Buster's coming," Cam groaned with a smile.

Camille smacked Cam's hand as she reached for a slice of fatback. "You are gonna have to wait like the rest of us. Why don't you and Sandy make an afternoon of it and bring us several catfish to fry? That way nobody should go hungry."

"We can do that."

Sandy returned to the kitchen. "Do what?"

"Catch up a mess of catfish to fry up with the boil. T's inviting Buster out, and you know how that boy can eat."

"Oh heck yeah, I love to fish."

Camille pointed at Cam. "You go hit the shower. Tell those sisters of yours to come set the table as you pass by their room, and you, *ma cherie*, go tell your papa to get ready for dinner. We'll be eating in twenty minutes."

"Yes, Mama," Sandy said and bolted out the back door.

Cam chuckled at Sandy's exuberance. She bent down and kissed her mother's cheek. "Love you, Mama."

"I love you too. Now git or you'll hold up dinner." She shooed her out of the kitchen and smiled. The five beautiful girls completed her and Ronny's dreams. Cam, Teresa, Karen, Wanda, and the baby Sandy kept them in stitches

7

with their antics, but each and every one of them had their own special skills to help keep the family businesses thriving.

†

Being the oldest did come with a few small privileges. Like a private room and a tiny bathroom all Cam's own. T, the next oldest, would take over her room in the fall when she left for college. Cam stripped out of her uniform and turned on the shower.

The warm water felt good on her skin, and when finished, she dried off and dressed in worn jeans and a tank top. After dinner, she'd slip a flannel shirt over the tank for the ride out to the Island. The full Louisiana summer had yet to arrive, so the night on the water could still be a bit on the cool side. Cam pulled on thick socks and her broken-in work boots, then ran her hands down her thighs. Her jeans were worn, and nearly see-through. She'd be lucky if they lasted the summer.

I reckon I'll have to break down and buy some new clothes for college. Wow, college. The word excited and terrified her at the same time.

She'd been away from home a few times for ball tournaments, and one spring break down at the coast. Sure, Baton Rouge wasn't that far away, but it was much larger than her little town, and there was so much a young, naïve country girl could get into in the big city that could get her bounced right back to Podunk.

She shook the negative thoughts from her head. She was determined to be successful and the first in their family to graduate from college. Cam opened her door to find Sandy with her hand raised, ready to knock.

"Dinner's ready. Mama says get a move on."

"Oh yeah?" Cam stepped out of her room and placed Sandy behind her. "Race you."

Sandy squealed, "You cheat," and did her best to pass Cam, who weaved down the hallway to block her until the very end when she let Sandy sneak by her. "I won," she cried out.

"This round, yes, but I'll get you next time."

Cam looked up to find her mama smiling at the exchange between sisters and winked at her. "She's a fast one, Mama. You're gonna have to keep an extra-close eye on this one when I'm gone." It was too late to take back her words, and Cam felt a twinge of guilt as she looked at Sandy, who was on the verge of tears. "Hey now, Squirt, I won't be gone forever. I'll come home every chance I get, and if you're lucky, I may get an extra ticket for a football game in Death Valley."

Sandy squealed. "Really, Cam?" Her disappointment temporarily forgotten, she slipped into a chair beside Cam.

Her dad walked into the room, his shoulders slumped with weariness. He smiled down at his oldest daughter. "Yak Box here said you hit another homer. What's that make, about twenty?"

"Twenty-two, and the state tournament is next week. Maybe I can add a few more to the record books before I graduate."

"Are the finals next weekend?"

"Yes, sir, on Saturday at the LSU field."

"Maybe we should load up the girls and go to the big city, Ma."

Camille carried a bowl of cabbage to the table. "That would be a nice break for all of us."

"Let's make it happen, then."

✝

The girls pitched in to clean the kitchen while their parents relaxed in the living room. Sandy carried the dishes from the table and sat on a stool watching as Cam and T washed and dried them while Wanda and Karen put away the leftovers.

T nudged Cam's shoulder. "Did I hear you say earlier that Bren was coming out tonight?"

"Yes, we're going over to the Island for a campfire at the hunt camp."

"You aren't gonna be sampling any of Dad's cooking, are ya?"

Heat rose up Cam's neck. "Probably not, I've got to be up early to help Dad and she's got to drive home."

T leaned in closer. "Y'all could stay out at the camp and get up early. No one would be the wiser."

"You have grown into such an instigator, Teresa St. Angelo," Cam teased. "Have you and Buster done that?"

T's face turned scarlet. There was no need to answer Cam's question. Her face revealed everything. "Only once, but we didn't stay all night."

"Uh-huh, you better not let Dad hear that or Buster may be in big trouble."

"He won't be the only one in trouble," Karen said as she bumped T with her hip. "You better keep those legs crossed, girlie."

"Will y'all relax? Buster's all hands and lips."

Wanda moved behind Sandy and covered her ears. "We all know what hands and lips can turn into quick," she said before Sandy wiggled out of her grasp.

"Will you stop, Wanda?" Sandy cried out.

"Sorry, Squirt, but some things you shouldn't be hearing yet," Cam said and shot a glare at Karen and Wanda.

10

Before anyone else could speak, a vehicle pulled up in the yard and Sandy rushed out of the kitchen to greet Bren.

"Slow down," Camille hollered from the living room as Sandy sped to the back door and slung it open.

Cam looked out the window to see Bren step out of the truck just as Sandy arrived. Her best friend ruffled Sandy's hair just as Cam had done so many times. Sandy reached for Bren's hand, and her mouth was moving ninety miles an hour as they walked to the house. Cam smiled at her baby sister's innocence and felt a twinge of jealousy at how easily Sandy took Bren's hand.

"Go ahead. We'll finish up here," Wanda told Cam after smacking her butt with the dish towel.

"Damn, ouch, that hurt. Tell Bren I'll be out in a minute. I've got to brush my teeth and get a flannel shirt."

Wanda nodded toward the yard. "No worries, I think Sandy will keep her busy for a few."

"It looks that way." Cam chuckled and left the room.

†

When Cam returned to the kitchen, Sandy was still talking ninety to nothing. "And Dad said he was going to load all us girls up and come watch y'all play in the finals next weekend."

"Whoa, slow down, Squirt. We've got to make it to the finals first."

"Cam, you know good and well you'll be there. No team has come close to beating y'all this year."

"That doesn't mean we can't have a bad day and lose."

Sandy cocked her head as she let Cam's words sink in. "I reckon that could happen."

Bren smiled sweetly at her. "We're going to do our best to make sure it doesn't happen, though."

11

"Darn straight we are." Cam looked at Bren. "Are you ready to head out?"

"Yes, I am." She hugged Sandy and kissed the top of her head. "See you next week, Squirt."

"Bye, Bren. You sure I can't go with you tonight, Cam?"

"Positive. Now get some sleep tonight so you can get up and help Dad and me with the cane so we can get out on the water sooner. We've got a big day tomorrow."

Cam walked into the living room to say good night to her parents. Ronny St. Angelo grinned at his daughter. "Go easy tonight. I put a six-pack of Abita's in the fridge if you'd rather have those. Make sure Bren's okay to drive before she leaves here. I'd rather she spent the night than end up in a ditch."

"Thanks, Dad." She leaned down to kiss his cheek. "We won't be out late, Mama."

"Just be careful."

"Yes, ma'am. See you bright and early, Dad."

"Good night, Cam."

CHAPTER TWO

Cam and Bren walked out to the boat they would take to the Island. "So, what's the grand adventure you have planned with Sandy tomorrow?"

"We're gonna round up some crawfish for a boil and catch a few catfish to fry up with them. T's invited Buster out, and you know that boy can eat."

"I bet she doesn't sleep a wink tonight. You know she worships you, right?"

"Yeah, but my baby sis has a crush on you, I think. Whenever she talks about you, she blushes."

Bren chuckled. "That's so sweet."

"It's going to break her heart when you marry Rudy. Mine too," she said without thinking.

Bren stepped into the boat and turned back to Cam. "I do believe that's the sweetest thing I've heard come out of your mouth, Cameron St. Angelo."

"It's true, but at least I'm losing you to a nice guy. If Rudy doesn't take good care of you, he'll have me and Sandy to contend with."

She waited until Cam stepped onto the board, then took a seat next to Cam. "He is a good guy. You will still be my best friend, Cam."

"Yeah, but things will change once you're an old married woman."

"Do I need to remind you that you're still a year older than me?"

"Ha, I'd have been graduated by now if Mama would have enrolled me in kindergarten on time."

Bren leaned against her as they pulled away from the docks. "I'm glad she didn't. It's been great having you in my life all these years."

"Yes, it has," Cam agreed as she opened up the throttle once they cleared the dock.

†

The family parcel on the Island had been in the St. Angelo family for hundreds of years. The hunt camp they had built there served a multitude of purposes. Not only a family getaway spot, the camp also served as a base for the private hunting trips her dad led each season. The Island was home to an abundance of white-tailed deer and wild boar. The trips helped supplement the family income from farming, harvesting gators, and the 'shine business her dad continued to run. The St. Angelo family, known to brew some of the finest 'shine in the South, used recipes handed down generation after generation. Yes, it was still illegal, but deep in the heart of Bayou Country, it was still a way of life.

Ronny and Camille were blessed to raise five female children. Cam, being the eldest, was the first tutored in the family business. She'd been helping her dad run the mash since she was twelve, and she proved a quick and apt student. It was with her dad's blessing that she developed the recipe for Red Bliss, a beautifully colored watermelon liquor, which quickly became popular. Ronny had said he could see the sparkle in his daughter's eyes as they cooked together, and he grew confident she would carry on the family business.

Cam maneuvered the boat through the narrow slough and pulled next to the dock. As the boat slowed, Bren picked up the mooring line and stepped onto the dock to tie off the boat. Darkness was falling quickly in the protected cove.

"I'll get a fire started if you'll grab a couple beers out of the cabin, unless of course you'd rather have 'shine."

"I have to drive home tonight, remember, so I'll stick to beer."

Cam watched her disappear inside the cabin, then turned to start a fire. She had laid a fire in the pit earlier in the week when she'd helped her dad with a run of Swamp Juice. All she needed to do was douse the stacked wood with a bit of diesel fuel and put a flame to it. A portable blowtorch was just the trick, and when Bren emerged from the cabin with two beers, the flames were licking through the pile of logs.

She handed Cam a beer. "It always amazes me how fast you can get a fire going."

Not as fast as you, but that's a different kind of fire. "I've had lots of time to practice over the years."

"I sure am going to miss these times when you go off to school."

"I imagine you'll be busy planning a wedding or some such thing," Cam said as she took a seat next to the fire.

"You'll be there. For the wedding, I mean."

Cam smirked. "I'll see what I can do."

"Would you consider being my maid of honor? You're my best friend and all. I think it's only right."

"You know I haven't worn a dress since they changed the dress code in second grade, to allow us to wear shorts and slacks as our uniforms in school."

"Really? The second grade."

"Yeah, me wearing a dress would be like a fish out of water. Maybe you could ask T or someone else who's into all that girly stuff. Besides, depending on your date, I probably wouldn't be able to be here for the rehearsals and all the events." Cam was relieved when Bren didn't appear to be upset with her. "I will be here for the wedding, no matter what." Bren held out her bottle and Cam gently tapped the neck of her bottle against it. "So when will you be planning the big event?"

"We were thinking about a Valentine's Day wedding, since that's when we first started dating."

Cam smiled. "That would be fitting. You think you'll still be able to wear white?"

"Hell yes! Rudy knows he's not getting anything until our honeymoon except a good case of blue balls."

Cam couldn't help but break into laughter at the comment. "That's going to make for one helluva honeymoon. Do you know where you want to go?"

"We'll probably go down to one of the beaches. Biloxi maybe, or Galveston."

"Rudy is starting out on the oil rigs this summer, isn't he? Are you going to be okay with two weeks on and two off?"

"Don't cherish the idea, but that's the best money Rudy can make. I've already got a job lined up at LB's, being a secretary at the processing plant. It's not glamorous, but it's money coming in."

Cam sensed a sadness come over Bren. "I'll still be seeing you when I come home to help Dad with the gators."

"Even if it is short weekends, it'll be good to see you."

"Maybe you and Rudy can come to town for a ball game or something when he's home."

16

"I'd like that." Bren took a long sip of her beer and sighed. "Where do you see yourself four years down the road, Cam?"

Cam fidgeted as she peeled the label from the bottle. "Honestly I have no clue. I can barely see past graduation at this point."

"Do you know what you want to study at LSU?"

"Not really, but the first year is basically core courses, so I won't have to declare a major right away."

"My, aren't we a pair?" Bren chuckled. "You ready?"

Cam drained the rest of the beer. "I am now."

†

Four more hours, they sat around the fire reminiscing about their childhood, laughing at some of the pranks they had pulled over the years. The wood had turned into glowing embers, allowing the darkness to close in around them.

Bren shivered. "You cold?"

"Naw, just a chill—a possum running over my grave, Granny would say. It is getting late, though, and you have a big day ahead. I know time's going to fly by after we graduate, but let's try to spend some time together before I head off to college."

"I'd like that very much, Cam."

"Let's make it happen, then," Cam said as she turned on a hose and doused the fire, filling the air with hissing smoke.

She denied being cold, but Bren snuggled in close to Cam as they rode back across the bayou. The reflection of the full moon shimmered on the water ahead, and the stars were specks of glitter as they filled the dark sky. Cam understood little of romance, but for a few moments, she wished the night with Bren would never end. They had shared so much, and tonight Cam realized both secretly

17

harbored apprehensions about the futures looming before them.

Strands of Bren's hair pulled away from her ponytail and blew against Cam's cheek as they neared the canal leading to her home. Cam smiled and wrapped an arm around her friend's shoulder, sharing the warmth of the fire burning in her heart.

After getting Bren off for home safely, Cam crept as quietly as possible into the house. It was just past midnight when she changed into her sleep clothes and crawled between the sheets. She tucked her head into the crook of her arm and a smile grew on her face as she breathed in the scent of Bren's perfume.

✝

Cam woke the next morning, ten minutes ahead of her alarm clock. She was enjoying the last few minutes of rest until the door clicked open and she peeked from the covers to see Sandy creeping into her room. She waited until Sandy was close enough to grab before lunging and pulling the squealing child into the bed. Cam placed her hand over Sandy's mouth. "Hush, you're gonna wake the dead."

Sandy settled onto the bed and snuggled into Cam's warmth. "You smell like Bren," she said with a suddenly sleepy voice.

"What?"

"Your arm, it smells like Bren's perfume."

Cam lifted her arm to her nose, and found the perfume lingering on her skin. "Yeah, it does. So why are you sneaking in here so early?"

"Mama's cooking pancakes and bacon for breakfast. She asked me to come get you to eat before Dad drags you off to the cane fields."

"I bet she said it just like that too, didn't she?"

Sandy nodded.

"How long have you been up?"

"I woke up about a half hour ago when I smelled the bacon cooking."

"We'd better hurry, then. If you smelled it, then so did our sisters. If we want bacon, we'd better go now."

"Can I still help you today?"

"Yes, ma'am, you can. Go get dressed and meet me in the kitchen."

Sandy leaned forward and kissed Cam's cheek. "Love ya."

"Love you more."

Sandy slid off the bed. "No way, man."

"Yes way, man."

Cam climbed from the bed and pulled on some work clothes, tied her hair back in a ponytail, washed her face, and brushed her teeth before walking to the kitchen. As she expected, Sandy was already sitting at the table, devouring a stack of pancakes. "Did you save some for me?"

"Mama's got a bunch just waiting on you."

Cam turned to find her mama handing her a plate with an equally large stack of pancakes and a mound of bacon. "Thanks, Mama."

"You want juice, milk, or both?"

"Both, please, so I can keep up with Squirt today."

"Wanda's going to drive the tractor for y'all while me and your other two sisters go grocery shopping. Is there anything special you'd like this week?"

"Will you make some banana-nut bread, please, Mom?"

"Sure. That does sound good, and I've got some overripe bananas."

"Is Dad already at the barn?"

19

"He's pulled out the tractor and is sharpening your cane knives. Do be careful with those things."

"I plan on coming back with everything intact, Mom."

"Watch the little one too and make sure she doesn't wander off chasing a butterfly or something."

Cam chuckled. "Yes, ma'am, I'll keep a close eye on her."

†

The morning sun was soon beating down on them as Cam and her dad cut the cane. They would cut the large stalks, and Wanda with Sandy's help would pile them onto a flatbed trailer. Ronny would deliver most of the harvest to the local farmers market, but they would hold back a portion to use in making Swamp Juice shine. It was a year-round favorite and a good source of income.

Cam stopped cutting the cane and wiped the sweat from her brow. Her dad, also taking a break, called out to her, "Let's get something cold to drink. It's hotter than a cat on a tin roof out here this morning."

"That it is. You'll get no argument from me."

Sandy ran back to the tractor and returned with ice-cold bottles of RC Cola for them. "Now if we only had a moon pie to go with these, it'd be darn near perfect," her dad said as he took a bottle from Sandy.

Cam took the bottle she offered. "Thanks, Squirt."

Ronny wiped his face on his shirtsleeve. "Two more rows ought to be good for today. I hear we're having a crawfish boil tonight."

"Yes, sir. The Squirt and I are gonna go get us some mudbugs and see if we can catch us a catfish or two. T's asked Buster out, so we gotta have plenty to eat."

"Ain't that the truth. I think your ma and I was blessed to have five girls. I can't imagine having to feed five growing boys."

Wanda chuckled. "You'd find a way, Dad. You always do."

"Thank goodness we have a bounty of food provided from the bayou. There have been some lean times for groceries, but we can always go catch or hunt what we need to live." He smiled at Cam. "I don't have to worry about you girls going hungry. You've got the skills to survive."

Cam returned his smile. "You've taught us well. We know more than how to thrive, but how to take from the swamp, to earn a living, and provide for others too. There are many families in town that depend on the goods we harvest."

"That's very true. This cane for instance will make some good syrup for someone to use or to sell to others for what they need." He drained his bottle. "So I guess we need to get back at it so we can get it to market and you and Sandy can get to fishing."

"All right," Sandy squealed.

Wanda climbed back onto the tractor. "I'll help Dad get the cane to the market so you two can get on the water."

Cam picked up her cane knife. "We'll all pitch in to get you loaded, and then we'll head out in the boat."

Sandy ran ahead of them and picked up a large stack of cut cane. "Slow your roll, Squirt. We've got plenty of time to fish."

"I know. I'm just so ready to go."

Cam chuckled and resumed cutting cane. In another thirty minutes, they were finished, loaded, and heading back home. After she saw the cane loaded in the truck, Camille called out to them, "I've got sandwiches on the table, so come and get them."

"I appreciate all your help."

"No problem, Dad. I enjoy working with you."

"I'm really gonna miss you when you're off at college."

"I won't be that far away and will be home every chance I get."

Ronny frowned. "I don't want that for you. I want you to enjoy your time at college without having to come home to work all the time."

"I promise I'll enjoy it, Dad, and I love working here too."

"I know, but life at college will be different and more challenging than high school. Remember, your education comes first."

"Yes, sir," Cam resigned, knowing she wouldn't win an argument with her dad. "Let's go eat."

"Now you're singing my tune," he said and walked inside the house with her.

†

Cam grinned as Sandy gobbled down a sandwich. "You know you should probably chew."

Sandy swallowed hard. "I'm just sooo ready, Cam."

"Okay, okay, I can take a hint." She grabbed a final sandwich and a glass of tea. "I reckon we'll see you all later."

"Be careful and bring us back some good stuff for dinner," Camille hollered as Sandy dragged Cam toward the back door.

CHAPTER THREE

Cam finished her sandwich on the way to the dock. She drank a sip of tea, pulled a battered LSU ball cap from her back pocket, and stepped onto the boat. She laced her ponytail through the back of the hat, checked to make sure they had rods and bait, then grinned at Sandy. "Cast us off, Squirt."

Sandy untied the line and pushed the boat away from the dock before stepping onboard.

"Let's go fishing. Then we can collect some mudbugs when we're done," Cam suggested.

"That sounds great to me," Sandy replied, wiggling in her seat.

Cam picked up her sunglasses to protect her eyes from the glare of the sun reflecting off the water as she steered them into a small channel that she knew would be a perfect spot to fish. She killed the motor and lowered an anchor into the water. "Bait 'em up, Squirt."

As soon as the boat slowed to a halt, Sandy picked up a rod and opened a container of beef melt Cam had prepared earlier in the morning. She wrinkled her nose at the pungent smell. "If a catfish can't smell this, they must be miles away from here."

"Oh, they'll smell it all right. Get that line in the water and let's see how long it takes."

Sandy cocked her head and looked at Cam. "You aren't going to fish?"

"Yep, just letting you get the little ones out of the way first."

Sandy chuckled and cast her line, and watched the bait disappear.

Cam kicked back in her seat, enjoying the intense concentration on her baby sister's face as she waited for a bite. She loved all her sisters, but Sandy was special to her. She never could quite put her finger on why, but she knew Sandy took up a large portion of her heart.

"I'm getting a nibble, Cam," she whispered loudly.

"Be ready to set the hook—oh hell yeah," she finished when Sandy expertly hooked the fish and she could tell from the bow in her rod that it wasn't a baby. "You got him now. Work him on in toward the boat and I'll get the net ready."

Sandy reeled in the line, and when Cam heard the gears of the reel grinding, she knew the fish was making a run. "Sit tight and let him wear himself out. When you feel the tension ease up, start reeling again." She knew there'd be a chance of escape if the fish made it to a grove of cypress knees, so Cam prayed he'd tire quickly. She was relieved when Sandy started to turn the crank again.

"He's coming along good now, Cam." Sandy's voice filled with excitement. Cam stood, picked up a net, and walked to where Sandy stood.

"He looks like a good one too," she said as the fish lunged through the surface briefly before diving. Beads of sweat had broken out across Sandy's brow. "Are you doing okay, Squirt?"

"Yep, I've got him."

"Yes, you do," Cam said as she dipped the net into the water, and with a loud swoosh, brought the fish onboard. "That's my girl," Cam called out as she ruffled Sandy's hair. "Grab the pliers out of the tackle box and let's get your hook back."

Sandy handed Cam the tool as the fish floundered on the floor of the boat, making a croaking sound, crying out his anger at being out of the water. She placed a booted foot to hold the fish while she extracted the hook from his gaping mouth. "Open the live well and we'll drop him in there."

"I can do it," Sandy proclaimed and took the net handle from Cam.

"Mind those whiskers. They can be painful if he catches you with one of them."

Sandy grinned up at her. "Yes, Mama."

"You'll be hollering for Mama if you get spiked."

Sandy carefully emptied the fish into the well and poured a bucket of water inside.

"Good job." Cam offered her a high five. "Now go do it again."

She returned to her comfortable seat to watch Sandy fish.

Sandy had landed five large fish and was baiting her hook, when Cam let out a low whistle. "Would ya look at that." She pointed toward the bank. "I do believe dat's Bubba Gump. Yep, there's his red spot," she said, leaning forward in her seat. The large gator was sunning himself on the bank, keeping a wary eye on the humans in the boat.

"Tell me about Bubba Gump, Cam," she pleaded.

Cam smiled at her baby sister. She had told her stories of Bubba Gump since Sandy was tiny. "He's probably the oldest gator in these parts, and hunters have tried to catch him since our dad was a little boy." Sandy sat still, enraptured by Cam's retelling of the story. "Dad will tell you that when he was a small boy, our Papi warned him the gator was the Boogeyman of da Swamp, and if kids were bad, they'd be dropped off in the swamp."

"What?" Sandy cried out.

"It's true." Cam leaned in closer. "There are many reports telling of a body needing to disappear that was dropped in the swamp, and Bubba Gump, and his kin, would make all the evidence…vanish without a trace."

"Cam, quit teasing me."

"I swear I'm telling God's honest truth. So, this Bubba Gump, he's a mean gator with a hunger for the taste of human flesh."

Cam held back her laughter as Sandy shivered at the thought.

"Hunters have been trying to capture him for a long time, but no one's ever managed to get him in da boat. Dat red spot on his head is a blemish from either a fight with another gator, or a hunter's bullet that missed the sweet spot. It's our way of telling him apart from the other large gators in da swamp. It can be scary at night, if you're out gigging frogs or riding the dark water to see those wicked yellow eyes in your spotlight and that red spot, glowing bright red."

"Have you or Dad ever tried to catch him?"

"Dad won't hunt for Bubba Gump. He still believes he's the Boogeyman of da Swamp, and won't even try for him. Says his hide is so tough and scarred up, it ain't worth a plug nickel. He has a great respect for him and the damage he can inflict."

Sandy stared at her, completely enthralled.

"You gonna fish or just sit there holding that stinky bait?"

Sandy chanced another glance at Bubba Gump and seemed pleased that he was still lazily sunning himself. She turned and cast her bait across open water to wait patiently for her next bite.

Cam knew the big gator could smell the bait and kept a close eye for any movement from him, intent to move along if he entered the water. *One day, big boy, we're gonna have a go at you.*

When Sandy landed the next fish, Cam decided they had enough for a good mess and pulled up the anchor. "Let's go get us some mudbugs," she told Sandy as she tucked away her rod. "You did so good catching our dinner, I didn't even have to pull out my rod."

Sandy beamed with pride at her praise, and Cam would make sure everyone around the dinner table tonight knew Sandy was the sole provider of the catfish. A quick glance at the bank revealed Bubba Gump feigning sleep, but Cam knew in an instant he could be active and strike at a target. They pulled up anchor and stowed the rods. She turned on the motor and turned the boat around to head into the canal by the hunt camp. There were crawdad traps farther down this canal, but Bubba was much too close for her comfort, so she picked another string of traps.

†

After emptying a line of traps, they had filled up five, five-gallon buckets.

"Ooh we, we gonna eat good tonight," Cam proclaimed as she dropped the trap back in the water after tossing a partially frozen fish head inside. She turned the boat in the direction of home and slowed. "I swear I'm plumb tuckered out. You wanna drive?"

"Heck yeah," Sandy answered as she flew out of her seat.

"Don't be a speed demon now. Just slow and steady until we get to the docks and I'll take her from there."

Cam sat back and watched her baby sister take over steering the boat. Sandy's strawberry-blonde hair had come loose from its ponytail and was blowing in the wind, and her face filled with a smile. Her mama frequently told her that Sandy was the spitting image of Cam when she was younger, and when they were out on the water, Cam could see the truth in her mother's words. Even though they were born ten years apart, they were alike not only in appearance, but in their mannerisms. Sandy's left hand drummed the console to an inner rhythm just as Cam's did when she steered the boat. She smiled and kicked her feet up for the short ride home.

†

As they approached the homestead, Cam smiled to see that Buster had arrived and he was helping her dad set up the cookers. *Man do I have a job for you.* Cam loved to fish, but she dreaded the task of skinning the six big catfish Sandy had caught. Since he would be eating a bunch of them, Cam felt it only right that Buster do the skinning.

"I'll take us in from here," she told Sandy, who slowed the boat to allow the shift of drivers. "You can get the mooring line ready and toss it to Buster when we dock."

Buster and her dad were walking down to meet them. Cam killed the motor and coasted toward the dock. Sandy tossed the line to Buster, who guided them close and tied the boat off.

"I had an idea on the ride home," Cam announced. "Since Sandy and I provided the fish and mudbugs for this feast, we see it only fitting that Buster has the honor of skinning the cats while we get cleaned up."

Buster broke out laughing. "I can handle that. Let's see what you got."

Sandy proudly opened the live well to show him the fish. "Six big ol' cats, and I got them all myself."

Ronny looked at Cam. "She sure did. She was on such a roll today, I didn't even have to wet a hook. You did good, Squirt. Those are some fine-looking cats and will make for some mighty fine eating."

"You made a good run on mudbugs too," her dad added.

"We shouldn't go hungry tonight, even with Buster here." Cam grinned.

"Hand those buckets of mudbugs up to me, and y'all can help me carry them up to the house while Buster gets started on the fish."

"That works for me," Buster said and began handing the buckets to Ronny.

"Better watch those whiskers," Sandy said, repeating Cam's earlier warning.

"I will, Squirt," Buster replied, and grinned up at her.

"I am so ready for a nice hot shower," Cam said as she climbed from the boat and stretched.

Ronny reached for the buckets of mudbugs. "Help me get these into a washtub and you're good to go." She and her dad took two of the buckets each. Sandy started to lift one until her dad saw her. "Leave it and I'll come back for it," he said. "You can run ahead and ask your mama for a pan and some buttermilk to soak those cats in once Buster finishes dressing and filleting them."

"Yes, sir," she hollered back over her shoulder as she left the boat and took off across the yard.

"Oh, to be that young and energetic," he chuckled. "Did she really catch all those fish?"

"Every last one of them. She was having too much fun for me to toss a line."

"Just like me and you used to."

"Yep, just like we used to do. I even got to introduce her to Bubba Gump today."

Her dad's smile turned to a scowl.

"Don't worry, he was sunning himself on the bank, but we decided we'd go run different traps for mudbugs. I had to tell her the Bogeyman of da Swamp story again."

"I still hate that damn gator."

"I know ya do, Dad. He makes for good entertainment, though."

Ronny chuckled. He emptied the first bucket into a large galvanized tub. "That he do."

"You got these?"

"Yes'm, run along and get you a shower."

"Thanks, Dad. See you in a bit."

†

Sandy was sitting outside her bedroom door when Cam emerged freshly dressed after a shower. "What's up, Squirt? Why are you sitting out here?"

"'Cause T and Wanda are hogging our bathroom," she pouted.

"Go get your clothes and you can use mine, then."

Sandy didn't need another invitation. She raced down the hallway to retrieve her clothes, leaving Cam laughing softly in her wake.

Cam walked into the kitchen and poured a glass of tea. Her mom was stirring up a batch of hush puppy mix.

"Will you hand me a can of beer, please?"

Cam pulled one from the fridge. "Is there anything else I can do to help?"

30

"Now that you mention it, you can open up some Ro-Tel, and whole-kernel-corn cans for me. Old man arthritis is giving me pains today."

"No problem, Mama." Cam pulled the canned goods from the pantry and made a mental note to use some of her graduation present money to buy her mama an electric can opener. Any of her sisters would assist her, but her mom detested having to ask for help, and her arthritis was getting worse.

Cam pulled out the crank can opener they had used for years, and for the first time realized how painful it must be for her mama as she opened two cans of each. "You want the corn drained?"

"Please, but not the Ro-Tel. I need the juice from them to help moisten the corn meal."

"You got it. You got enough onions chopped?"

"T did those for me earlier. She left here with tears running down her cheeks."

"Better her than me." Cam carried the cans over to her. "I'm going to check on the boys to see how they're doing getting those cookers set up. You need anything else before I go?"

"No, but you can take your dad one of those cold beers and ask Buster to come carry the cooler out."

"Yes, ma'am, will do. Let me know when you've got the hush puppy batter ready and I'll carry it out. You know, I think it's time to teach Sandy how to cook 'em."

"Teach me how to cook what?" Sandy asked as she towel-dried her hair on the way down the hall.

"You wanna help me cook hush puppies?"

"Oh, heck yeah," she squealed.

"Go finish getting ready, then."

Cam smiled as Sandy raced back down the hall, and looked over to see her mama smiling at her.

31

"It's going to be a toss-up, you know."

"What is?"

"For who misses you most once you go off to college, between me, your dad, or Sandy."

Cam wrapped her arms around her mama from behind. "I'm going to miss all of you, but you most. You're the best friend I've ever had."

Camille continued to knead the batter. "You'll have plenty more friends once you go off to school."

She hugged her gently, "Maybe so, but none like my mama."

"Go now, before you get me crying."

Cam leaned down to kiss her cheek. "Love ya, Mama."

"Love you too. Don't forget to take your dad a beer."

"Got it." Cam plucked two beers from a tub full of ice. *Buster can get his own when he comes to get the tub.* She smiled as she stepped out into the late spring day.

Three cookers were arranged around the fire pit. Her dad would prepare the crawfish boil in one, T would fry the catfish in another, and Cam would teach Sandy the fine art of making hush puppies in the third. T had already started both fryers to get the oil heating.

"Won't be long now," she said when Cam walked up and handed her dad a beer.

"Where's mine?" Buster asked.

"It's still in the tub full of ice with the rest of the cold drinks, waiting for you to bring them down."

"I reckon I can take a hint. I'll be back in a minute," he said and kissed T on the top of her head.

Wanda and Karen were spreading sheets of heavy plastic over the tables beneath the pavilion. The back door flew open before Buster arrived, and Sandy barreled out carrying four rolls of paper towels.

"Whoa der, li'l one, you betta slow dat roll," Buster teased as she breezed past him.

She laid the paper towels on the nearest table and rushed over to Cam. "Mama says the batter is ready if you wanna come get it."

"Let's do it, then. We need to get a head start on cooking anyhow."

They arrived at the back door in perfect timing to hold it open for Buster before returning to the kitchen.

"I've got you a couple of tablespoons, your big dipping spoons, and some pans to drain your pups," their mama said.

"I'll get the batter if you can get everything else," Cam told Sandy.

"No problem." Sandy took the pans Camille offered her.

"Sit for a spell and come on down when you're ready, Mama."

"I think I will, Cam. Be careful around that grease, Squirt, and listen to what Cam tells ya."

"Yes, Mama," Sandy answered.

Cam picked up the large bowl of hush puppy batter and started singing, 'Who Let the Dogs Out?'

Sandy came in just in time to sing, "Woof, woof, woof, woof."

†

Camille laughed at her daughters' antics and dried off her hands. She welcomed a few minutes of peace and quiet before the cooking started in earnest. She glanced out the window and watched her brood at work as they prepared for the night's feast. *I'm truly a blessed woman to have such a fine family.* She picked up her glass of sweet tea and walked to the living room to sink down in the comfortable easy

33

chair. She pulled the handle to raise the footrest and closed her eyes to relax.

†

Cam pulled up two stools close to their cooking station. Sandy crawled on top of hers to listen to what Cam was telling her. She watched Cam remove a thermometer from the heating oil.

"Just perfect," she said as she placed the thermometer on the table. "The first step to cooking hush puppies is to carefully drop the batter in the oil without sloshing oil everywhere, burning yourself, and catching stuff on fire."

"Should I go get a fire extinguisher?" Buster teased.

"Nope, Squirt's a good student and will do just fine."

Sandy smiled at the praise.

"I'll use a tablespoon to dip out some of the batter and make it into a small ball. When it's rounded, I'll take my finger and carefully push the batter off the spoon into the oil," she said, demonstrating the technique. "I'll drop 'em if you'll dip 'em and hand me the spoons." Cam was afraid Sandy wasn't tall enough to safely place the hush puppies in the grease just yet. "Once we get a good batch going, you can dip them out when they're a nice golden-brown. Sound like a plan to you?"

"I'm on it," Sandy said and took the spoon Cam had used. She filled it with batter and handed it to her.

"Now use the other tablespoon while I drop this one."

They alternated spoons until the surface of the cooker was filled with hush puppies. As they began to float to the top, Cam turned them over to cook the other side. "In just a few more seconds, they will be done and you'll need to start dipping them out. Sit up on your knees on the stool so you can see." Cam waited for Sandy to adjust her position. "Now, just like we dipped those catfish out today, you're going to use the big slotted spoon to dip them out and place them in the pan with paper towels lining it to let them drain. Go slow so the oil doesn't go everywhere." Cam put a potholder on her right hand and held the cook pot as Sandy carefully pulled out the first batch of hush puppies. "Good job," she told her before taking a long drink of her beer. "Now we drop more."

T and Wanda were cooking the catfish fillets, and when they had a sizeable mound prepared, their dad called out to Buster, "I reckon we'd better get to cooking too. Help me with this basket."

They watched as Buster and Ronny lifted a ten-gallon basket of crawfish, potatoes, and corn on the cob, and placed it inside the cooker filled with boiling water. A few drops of water erupted from the pot, hissing as they hit the flame.

"We got it going on now," Ronny cried out when the basket reached the bottom.

Cam was surprised when she looked up from cooking that her mama hadn't joined them yet. "Go check on Mama, please, Wanda. I would have thought she'd have come down by now."

Wanda nodded. "Sure thing, Cam."

Cam looked at Sandy. "Let's try out your hush puppies."

They each made a selection from the first batch that had cooled and took a bite.

"Mm-mm, I think these may be the best ever," Cam said after she swallowed.

"They are good, huh?"

"Yes, ma'am, they are. You want to pass some around?"

Sandy nodded and Cam watched with pride as the young girl climbed down from her stool and carefully carried a pan of the cooked hush puppies around to each of their family for a sample. She was quick to warn Buster the piece he was going for was still too hot, and giggled when he dropped it quickly back onto the pan and made another selection.

†

Wanda entered the house, and when she walked into the living room, she saw her mama sleeping peacefully in the recliner. For a moment, she was tempted to let her sleep and bring her a plate of food when it was done, but she knew Camille would be disappointed at missing the family fun. So she knelt next to her, gently shook her arm, and softly whispered, "Mama, it's time to wake up."

Camille jerked wide-awake, sending Wanda tumbling backward. "What the heck?" She looked to her right at Wanda on the floor. "What are you doing down there?"

"I thought I'd check for cracks in the tiles," she replied with a grin.

"What?"

"You startled me when you woke so suddenly, and I fell backward."

"I'm sorry, honey. I didn't hit you, did I?"

"No, Mama, you didn't. You were sleeping pretty good, though. Cam asked me to come check on you. It won't be long before the food is ready."

"I didn't realize I would drift off like that."

"We've all been working hard, Mama. A little nap didn't hurt you any."

Camille dropped the footrest and leaned forward. "Let me wash my face and I'll be right out."

"Okay, Mama. Is there anything else that needs to go out?"

"You might wanna take out some hot sauce, and tartar sauce for the fish if someone hasn't already gotten it."

"I'll check on my way back through. Love ya, Mama."

"Love you too, honey. Oh yeah, grab that cheese sauce Cam likes on her hush puppies too, please. It's on the top shelf in the fridge."

"Got it."

†

After everyone got their fill of food, they sat around the fire pit enjoying the beautiful night. Sandy had snuggled up with Cam as she pointed out various constellations to her baby sister. The warmth of her smaller body was comforting to Cam, and she draped an arm around Sandy's shoulder.

"Look," she said, pointing out a shooting star. "Make a wish." She smiled as Sandy squeezed her eyes shut and remained silent.

When Sandy opened them, she was frowning.

"What's wrong?"

"I made a selfish wish. Is it too late to take it back?"

"No wish is ever wrong."

"This one was." Sandy had tears in her eyes as she looked up at Cam. "I wished you didn't have to go away."

Emotion choked off the words before Cam could speak, and her eyes grew wet. When she was able to speak, she leaned closer to Sandy. "Sometimes I wish that too, but I know in my heart this is something I need to do. Dad and Mama are dead set on me graduating from college."

"I know, but I'm going to miss you so bad."

"I'm going to miss you too, Squirt, but I won't be far away, and I promise to come home as often as I can. You can even come visit for the weekend sometime too."

"Really, Cam?"

"I don't see why not." She held her close. "Love ya, Squirt."

"Love ya more."

"Nope, no way, man," Cam replied and started tickling her sister.

"Do too," she squealed between giggles.

CHAPTER FOUR

The last few weeks of her high school years sped by. The team won state, Cam received the award for Most Valuable Player of the tournament, and she added several more home runs to the high school record books. They played Bugsy's team for the championship and beat them by two runs. Cam had played well and added another homer to her record. After the game, they had lined up for the traditional handshake, and as Cam was shaking hands with one of Bugsy's teammates, Bugsy bumped into her from behind with her shoulder.

"Way to impress our new coach with that homer. I bet it felt good to know you can hit one out of this ballpark."

"I have to admit, Bugsy, it did feel good."

Bugsy wiggled her eyebrows at Cam. "Maybe we'll luck up and become roommates and I can show you what else can feel good."

Cam looked straight into her eyes. "Never gonna happen, Bugsy. You're not my type."

"We'll see about that. I've watched how you look at other players. You can't deny that you're not interested."

"In others possibly, but not you, Bugsy. It will be great to be on the same team, but teammates is all we'll ever be." Cam was irritated with Bugsy's flirtations.

Bugsy glared at her fiercely. "We'll see about that. See you soon, Cam."

Cam was glad Bugsy turned away and walked toward the dugout. She was a good ballplayer, but something about Bugsy just creeped her out.

†

After the tournament, the LSU coach came by to congratulate Cam on the win and to introduce her to one of the star players, second baseman Tab Fortner.

"Welcome to the team, rookie." Tab beamed. "You've hit the bonanza. You're going to be my roomie next fall."

Cam looked at the coach. She nodded. "I like to pair up new players with a seasoned athlete to help show you the ropes, and hopefully keep you out of the trouble college life can bring. I'm not so sure about pairing the two of you up, though." She grinned. "Tab insisted on picking you out of next year's freshman crop."

"I should be honored, then." Cam placed her hand over her chest and bowed from the waist.

"See, Coach, we're going to get along just fine." Tab winked.

"That's what I'm afraid of. You're two of a kind. Double the trouble."

"Aww, Coach, you settled me down pretty good."

"Yeah, so do you hold the record for extra laps?"

Tab gave Cam a crooked grin. "How'd you know?"

Coach groaned. "Dear Lord, what have I gotten myself into here?"

"Here's my number. I'm from Monroe, but maybe sometime this summer we can get together and plan the mayhem we're going to cause next year."

"I did not hear that. See you soon, Cam. Stay in good shape." Her new coach spun on her heels and walked away, the young girls in the stands clamoring for her autograph as they circled around her.

"Have a great summer and I'll see you soon," Tab said.

"Sounds great," Cam answered and went to find her family. She heard Sandy squealing and saw her waving madly from the stadium bleachers. She smiled and took the steps two at a time.

"You were awesome, Cam."

She grabbed Sandy up and spun with her in her arms. "The team looked great today, didn't we?"

"Yes, and that homer you hit was fantastic."

"You're biased, but I'm glad you were here. All of you," she added as she turned to the rest of the family.

Her dad grinned. "We'll see you at home later tonight. Now go celebrate with your team."

"Love y'all," she said as she put Sandy down on the bleacher steps. "Be careful driving home."

†

She climbed onto the bus and was delighted to see that Bren had saved the seat beside her.

"Hey, hot stuff. I saw you talking with Coach. Is everything okay?"

"Yeah, she congratulated us for our win and introduced me to my roommate for next year."

"You mean that gorgeous woman that was with her?"

41

Cam nodded. "Tab Fortner, her second baseman. Coach thinks she can show me the ropes to campus life and hopes she can keep me outta trouble."

Bren laughed. "You can't be serious. She looks like she could be quite a handful. Add your mischievous nature and look out, Baton Rouge."

Cam stowed her bag under the bench and slipped into the seat beside Bren. "Only time will tell."

✝

Graduation was an eventful time, and numerous parties were held to celebrate the ending of childhood and the first step into the adventure of adulthood. Cam and Bren tried to get together often, but Bren's new job limited the time they had together. As August approached, they shared a night on the Island.

Bren turned in her chair to look at Cam. "I'm going to miss these times together."

"You'll be busy planning a wedding and I'll be off at school, but I'll never forget the times we've shared," Cam promised.

"You'll still come for the wedding, right?"

"I wouldn't miss it for the world."

Bren surprised her by leaning in and softly kissing her lips. "I hope you find what you're looking for in Baton Rouge."

"I've got to figure out what that is first." Cam looked at her with the lopsided grin Bren loved.

Bren giggled. "Look out, Baton Rouge."

✝

42

Cam spent her summer working beside her dad, Sandy tagging along to help where she could. Cam made a special point of taking time out to spend with Sandy, usually out on the open water they both loved. Her dad kept his promise and had her Jeep painted as part of her graduation present, and when he brought it home, the sleek black vehicle looked brand new.

"I think you need to take her on a road trip," he announced when he tossed her the keys.

"Where do you think I should go?"

"Well, seeing as how you have a hotel reservation in Grand Isle tomorrow night, I think that would be a good spot. Drop the top and let the wind blow in your hair. In a few weeks, you're going to be busier than a one-armed paper hanger."

Cam looked down at Sandy, glued to her side. "What do you say, Squirt? Are you up for a road trip?"

"Oh heck yeah," she squealed. "You'd really take me?"

"There's no one else I'd rather be with. Guess we need to go pack a bag so we can leave early in the morning."

Sandy took off running back toward the house, still squealing.

"That was very nice of you," her dad said as he draped an arm across her shoulders.

"Thank you for giving us this opportunity."

"You've more than earned it. I just wish I could afford to let you stay longer."

"Trust me, Dad, we'll make the most of it."

"I'm sure you will. Your mama plans on sending sandwiches with you, so if she doesn't know by now, she needs to plan for two. I've got gas money and a little spending money put back for you too."

Cam stopped, turned to him, and hugged him tight. "Love you, Dad."

"I love you too. Let's go see if we can peel the little one off the ceiling and see what your mama is cooking for supper."

†

When they walked into the kitchen, Camille was stirring a pot of spaghetti sauce. "What on earth did you do to Sandy? She came through here like her hair was on fire, yelling something about packing her bags."

Ronny chuckled. "Cam's going to take her on her road trip."

"That certainly explains her excitement. That's sweet of you, Cam."

"It'll be fun and a great memory for both of us."

"You two go get cleaned up for supper. It'll be ready in about five minutes."

"Yes, Mama."

As she walked past the room Sandy shared with her sisters, Cam peeked inside. Sandy had pulled out a small suitcase and was sorting through her clothes. Cam leaned against the doorframe. "You only need one outfit. It's just one night, so travel light."

"I will, Cam."

Cam walked on to her bedroom and cleaned up for supper. She pulled out a small duffle bag and tossed it on her bed. She would pack after supper and get her dad to share his road atlas with her so she could plan her route. She heard the pounding of small feet on the wood floor and knew Sandy was on her way down the hall.

Sandy skidded to a halt just outside her door. "Mama said get a move on, it's time to eat."

"You don't have to tell me twice." Cam followed her from the room.

44

†

"That was a great meal, Mama," Cam said as she pushed her plate away.

"I'm glad you liked it. What kind of sandwiches do you want me to pack for you?"

"Would you mind packing us a fresh loaf of white bread and a half dozen of your tomatoes? We can stop and pick up a small jar of mayo, some chips, and some of those picnic salt and pepper shakers."

"A cooler of sodas too," her dad chimed in.

"That's way too easy. How about some ham biscuits to take with you? I'm not sure Sandy will sleep tonight, so you'll probably roll out at the crack of dawn."

Cam stood to carry her dishes to the kitchen. "We might as well take advantage of the daylight while we can." She winked at Sandy.

"That's my girl. I've got a route mapped out for you already. Just follow the yellow highlighter mark."

"Is that anything like "follow the Yellow Brick Road"?"

Sandy giggled. "Cam, you're so funny."

She shrugged with a smile. "I guess we're not in Kansas."

Wanda pushed out her bottom lip. "You guys are going to have so much fun. I'm jealous."

Cam ruffled Wanda's hair as she passed by. "We'll be sure to tell you all about it."

"That makes me feel so much better," Wanda teased.

"You go ahead with your dad to look at that map. Your sisters and I will clean the kitchen."

†

While she and her dad reviewed the map, they heard the tapping of raindrops on the tin roof.

"Don't worry, it'll be gone by the morning."

"Good, I hate driving in the rain."

"The next few days look clear, so you should be good to go."

"That sounds great. Thanks again, Dad."

"You've earned it, honey. Just wish it was more."

"It's a perfect getaway. Wish everyone could go."

"Maybe one day we'll all take a nice vacation."

"That would be nice."

"You should probably finish packing and get some sleep. Sandy's gonna get you up early."

"Yep, true dat."

"Good night, Cam. See you in the morning."

"Good night, Dad. Thanks again for everything." She bent down to kiss his cheek and left the room.

She packed her bag, prepared for bed, and climbed beneath the cool sheets. Lightning flashed outside her window and lit up the stormy bayou. Cam closed her eyes and let the pounding of the raindrops on the tin roof call her to sleep.

CHAPTER FIVE

The rain had passed through during the night, and the sun hadn't risen yet when Sandy bounced onto Cam's bed. "Wake up, sleepyhead." She poked Cam in the ribs.

"Is it morning already?" Cam groaned.

"It's almost six," Sandy jabbered. "Mama's got the biscuits and ham finished and our cooler is packed too. Dad's already carried it out to the Jeep."

"Damn, I guess I'd better get a move on before you leave without me."

"You know I can't reach the pedals, Cam."

"Good thing or I might be walking. Go help Mama finish up and I'll be right there."

Sandy raced from the room as Cam climbed from the bed and walked to the bathroom. One look in the mirror made her grimace at her case of bedhead. *Nothing my ball cap won't hide.* She grinned as she wet her hair and pulled it back into a ponytail, then washed her face and brushed her teeth.

She picked up her bag and walked into the kitchen.

"Finally," Sandy squealed, grabbed her bag, and bolted out of the house.

Her mama looked up and smiled at Sandy's excitement. "I don't think she slept much."

"Apparently not, but she's full of energy."

"Her first road trip and with her hero to boot, so what do you expect?"

"I expect we're going to have a great time."

Her dad walked in from outside. "All you need is the ham and biscuits and you're ready to go."

Her mama handed her a thermos of coffee and a travel mug. "I think you're going to need this."

"Please tell me you didn't pack any caffeine for Squirt?"

"Nope, she's already got a bottle of apple juice in the console. She's just waiting on you."

Cam chuckled and took the coffee, and her mama picked up the bag of biscuits.

"I already rolled your top down," her dad said as they walked her outside.

"I reckon we're good to go."

"There's an envelope in the glove box with cash for gas, food, and the hotel. Y'all have a great time," he told her as they walked to the Jeep.

Sandy had already climbed inside and had her seat belt fastened.

"Did you kiss Mama goodbye?" Cam asked.

"Dang, I knew I was forgetting something." Sandy unfastened her seat belt, and jumped down to hug and kiss her parents.

"You two have a great time and come back safely," Camille said.

"We will, Mama."

Cam hugged her parents. "See you soon," she said and walked around to climb in the Jeep.

She cranked the vehicle and pulled away slowly, watching her parents in the rearview mirror as they smiled and waved. She tossed up her hand in a wave and turned left onto the road. "Here we go, Squirt."

A smile filled Sandy's face as the sun crept above the horizon. Cam had studied the map and knew the route she was taking, so she relaxed and enjoyed the cool morning breeze. When the sun rose, she reached into the console to take out a pair of sunglasses and handed Sandy a smaller pair. She had to admit, they looked cool with the top down, their dark shades on, and their hair blowing in the wind. She smiled back at Sandy, who was glowing with excitement.

She took a sip of her coffee and asked Sandy to pull them out a biscuit. Sandy handed her a thick biscuit stuffed with ham. "Thanks." She grinned and took a bite. "Oh, hell yeah," she said after swallowing. "I sure am gonna miss our mama's cooking."

A frown came to Sandy's face. "Can we please not talk about you going away?"

She chuckled. "Sure, baby sis. I'm sorry."

"I just don't want to think about it and spoil our fun."

"I understand completely."

†

A few hours later, they stopped for a break in La Place, just outside of New Orleans, to top off the gas tank.

"Do you want to stop for lunch or keep driving?"

"Let's keep going, Cam. How much farther until we get there?"

"Maybe two hours tops. Why don't you go use the restroom while I fill the tank, and then I'll come in and use the restroom? You can find us a bag of chips and a small bottle of mayo."

49

"Deal," Sandy answered and bounded out of the Jeep.

Cam reached inside the glove box for a couple of twenties and then locked the compartment. She topped off the tank and walked inside to pay. Sandy had located a small squeeze bottle of mayo and was studying the rack of chips. Cam handed her a ten and a set of picnic salt and pepper shakers. "I'll be right back."

When she returned from the restroom, Sandy was waiting for her at the counter, holding the bag of supplies.

"All set?"

"Yes, ma'am."

Cam took the bag and placed the mayo in the cooler before storing the chips and seasoning. "Do you want a drink while I'm back here?"

"I'll take a Coke."

Cam pulled out a can of Coke and a bottle of water. "Here you go, Squirt."

When she pulled back onto the interstate, Cam wondered if Sandy had ever been this far south. They were starting across the long bridge spanning Lake Pontchartrain and her head was swiveling from side to side as she looked out at the refineries and the large expanse of the lake.

"This is one big lake, isn't it?" she asked, grinning.

"Yeah, it is. Seems like it goes on forever."

A few minutes later, Sandy gasped and pointed out the windshield. "Is that the Superdome?"

"Yep, dat's the home of the Saints," Cam answered as she took the exit to bypass New Orleans. Maybe they would venture downtown on the way back if time permitted.

They started across a large metal bridge. "Wow, is this the Mississippi? It's so much bigger here."

"You're just up higher so you can see more of it," Cam chuckled as Sandy sat, amazed by the Big Muddy.

Sandy's excitement made Cam glad she'd decided to bring her baby sister along for the trip. As soon as they cleared New Orleans, they passed endless fields of sugarcane as they drove through small towns, moving ever closer to the coast. When Cam smelled salt in the air, she knew they were getting close to Grand Isle. The swampy land and cane fields suddenly opened to the beautiful coastline, the sun glittering off the blue water. Cam knew from studying the map that there was a state park that would be a great spot for them to spend the afternoon and have their lunch. When she saw the sign advertising the park, she turned left, paid the small entrance fee, and drove along the Gulf until she found a remote covered picnic table. *Perfect.*

"Let's have some lunch, and then we can take a walk down the beach."

"Good, I'm starved."

Cam parked and unloaded the bags of food and the cooler they would need for lunch. She smiled when she opened the cooler for the mayo and found that her mama had already sliced the tomatoes for their sandwiches. She had even packed paper plates and a roll of paper towels.

"Mama set us up good," she said as she laid out their picnic.

A flock of seagulls approached, hoping for a handout, and Cam handed Sandy the heel and several slices of bread to occupy them while she prepared the sandwiches. Sandy giggled as she walked out to the light brown sand of the beach and tore off bits of bread to toss to the ravenous birds. They raised quite a commotion as they fought for the scraps Sandy flung into the air. After they devoured her offering and she had nothing left, they flew farther down the coast in search of more food.

"Man, they sure were a noisy bunch," Cam said as Sandy returned.

"Hungry too," she said as she brushed her hair back from her face.

"Pour us some chips on our plates and grab us a soda while I finish these sandwiches."

"You got it."

Cam smiled as Sandy pulled out a bag of BBQ potato chips and sprinkled them onto their plates. They were Cam's favorite and Sandy loved them too. She grabbed two cans of Coke from the cooler and placed them on the table as Cam set a plate mounded with tomato sandwiches between them.

"Those look great."

"Go ahead and dig in. We've got plenty more if we need them."

Cam sat across from her and picked up half a sandwich. She was about to take a bite when she spotted a large ship on the water. "Look, a cruise ship."

Sandy's head spun around and she squinted against the sun's rays. "Where do you think they're going?"

"Probably Mexico, from the direction they're headed."

"I'm not sure I'd want to be on a big ship with all those strangers."

"I'm not either. I think it'd be too easy to become bored," Cam confessed. "I guess the people you are with would make all the difference, though."

"You and I could have fun, I bet."

"We have fun wherever we go. Maybe one day we'll go on a cruise together."

"It'd sure be a lot different than an airboat on the swamp."

Cam chuckled. "Yes, it would be much different. Eat up."

"I'm glad you invited me on your trip. I needed this time with you." Sandy had a sadness in her voice.

Cam sometimes had to remind herself of Sandy's age, but there was an old soul in that young child's body, and she came out with some wisdom beyond her years from time to time. "There's no one else I'd rather share this adventure with."

Sandy beamed as she took another sandwich from the pile and bit into the middle, the ample mayo squirting out the corner of her mouth. Her tongue swiped across her lips and she grinned at Cam.

When they finished the sandwiches, they packed up their supplies. "You ready for a walk on the beach?"

"Ready when you are." Sandy kicked off her shoes and placed them on the bench.

Cam took off her shoes and walked around to join her. "Which way should we go?"

Sandy reached up and took her hand. "Let's go this way."

Cam enjoyed the feel of Sandy's small hand in hers and allowed her to choose the direction and speed that they would walk. She was secretly disappointed when Sandy released her hand to chase after the water as it raced back from the shore.

"Wow, it's warm," she called back to Cam.

Cam joined her at the water's edge and waded out. "You're right, it is."

Sandy raced ahead, water splashing up from her footsteps. As she bent over, Cam craned her neck to see what her sister had found. When Sandy turned and raced back toward her, she held a perfectly formed sand dollar in her little hand. "Look, a sand dollar."

Cam leaned over to inspect the object. "Not even a crack in it. Since we're close, why don't you take it back to the table and grab one of those empty plastic bags in case you find other treasures?"

"I'll be right back," she answered and raced to the picnic table.

Cam waded through the warm water, marveling at the variety of shells uncovered by the surf's movement. She picked up several tiny shells and held them out to Sandy when she returned.

"Those are pretty," she said as she took them from Cam and placed them inside the bag.

When they reached a large driftwood log, Cam sat and watched Sandy hunting for treasure. She held the plastic bag, allowing Sandy to continue her search with both hands free. Cam looked into the bag, inspecting the shells and small fragments of coral that had washed onshore from God knows where. She glanced up at Sandy and smiled. The sunlight played on her golden hair, which seemed to glow in the afternoon light. Strands had escaped her ponytail and she brushed them back as the breeze blew them into her face. *She's so sweet and innocent. I can't remember those days.*

Sandy pounced on another treasure as the water receded and looked up to find Cam watching her. She picked up a small starfish and rushed over to Cam. "Look."

"Wow, that's a great find!"

The tiny feet moved against Sandy's palm and she giggled as it tickled her.

"You know he's still alive and if you take him, he will die, right?"

Sandy's head jerked up and she had a frown on her face. "I didn't think of that." She turned and raced back into the water and gently placed the starfish on the sand, then waited for the surf to draw him deeper. She ran back over to Cam. "There, that's done."

"Good decision." Cam cocked her head and looked at Sandy. Her expression must have puzzled the girl, because Cam's forehead was wrinkled up in a frown.

"What's wrong?"

"Nothing's wrong, but did you have those freckles when we arrived?"

"These you mean?" She pointed to a sprinkling of freckles across her nose and under both eyes. "Yes, silly, I've had them forever."

"I reckon I've just never noticed them until now."

Cam stood and walked farther down the beach as Sandy played in the surf. She stopped when she saw a large clear ball-like creature washed up on the beach. "Sandy, come here, please," she said as she bent over it.

Sandy ran over to her. "What is it?"

"It's a jellyfish. See these tentacles? If they wrap around you, they will sting you like crazy, so be careful in the water. They are so clear, you don't see them until it's too late."

"Like a bee sting?"

"Yeah, but a hundred times worse, so be careful."

"I will, Cam, I promise."

Cam continued her stroll, and when she found two more jellyfish within the next twenty-five yards, she felt it was time to get Sandy out of the water. She was turning to call for her, when she heard Sandy squeal. Her heart pounded as she rushed toward her sister, who was holding her arm, running as fast as she could in the knee-deep water.

"I'm sorry, Cam, I was chasing a small fish and didn't realize the jellyfish was there," she cried.

"It's going to be okay, honey. Let me see."

Sandy removed her hand from her wrist, where a small welt was already forming. Cam studied it closely and could see a few tiny tentacles attached to the skin. "Time for some first aid," she said and picked Sandy up and hurried back to the picnic table. "Sit tight and I will be right back, okay?"

Sandy nodded as tears flowed down her cheeks. Cam rushed to the back of the Jeep and pulled out her bag. She opened her hygiene kit, took out a can of shaving cream, then rummaged further until she found an alcohol wipe. She raced back to Sandy and pulled her pocketknife from her shorts. Sandy's eyes grew wide when she saw it.

"You're not going to cut me, are you?"

"Heavens no," Cam answered. "Let me see your arm."

Sandy held it out and watched as Cam spread shaving cream over the welt, then placed the can on the table. She opened her knife and used the top edge of the blade to scrape the shaving cream and the tentacles from the skin. Cam flung the cream from her blade and placed the knife on the table. She tore the top off the alcohol wipe packet, opened it, and covered the welt with the cool wrap.

"That feels better already," Sandy said.

Cam sat beside her and wiped the tears from her cheeks. "I'm sorry. I shouldn't have let you go back in once we saw the first one."

"No, Cam, I didn't listen well enough to your warning, and I wasn't paying attention like you said."

"Well, at least it's not a huge sting, but I bet it still hurts plenty."

"You were right about the hundred times worse than a bee sting."

"Hopefully it will begin to ease up some. I'll get our stuff packed and we can find a pharmacy to get some vinegar and Benadryl."

"Eww, why vinegar? That stuff stinks."

"Yes, it does, but it will help to draw the sting out and make it feel better."

Cam rushed to put their picnic supplies in the Jeep and grabbed their shoes before picking Sandy up and carrying her to the Jeep.

She used an old towel to wipe the sand from Sandy's feet and slipped her shoes on, then did the same for herself. She climbed into the Jeep and drove as quickly as possible out of the park. When she found a chain pharmacy and pulled into the parking lot, she grabbed the envelope of cash and looked at Sandy. "Will you be okay out here while I go in?"

"Yes, silly. Go on already."

"Smart aleck," Cam teased and rushed inside the store.

She found a bottle of vinegar and a package of Benadryl and went to the pharmacy counter. The woman behind it looked at her and asked, "Jellyfish sting?"

"Yes, ma'am. Is there anything else I need?"

"Grab a tube of that itch cream on the second shelf on the wall. How bad and where?"

"On her wrist about two inches long. She's only eight."

"Have you treated it with anything yet?"

"Shaving cream to get the rest of the tentacles, and an alcohol swab."

The woman smiled. "That was very ingenious. This should do the rest of the trick. Give her some Benadryl, but don't be alarmed if she goes to sleep. Soak the wrist in vinegar for a few minutes, and when it's dry, apply the anti-itch cream."

"I need something to soak her wrist in."

"No worries," the woman said and pulled out a large Ziploc bag used for carrying medicine bottles. "Use this. It'll work like a charm and is easy to dispose of. Good luck."

"Thanks," she said and rushed from the store.

"We're gonna have you all set in just a few minutes," Cam said when she reached the Jeep. She pulled open the bag and poured half the bottle of vinegar inside.

"Eww, that really stinks."

"I know, but I promise it will help. Put your hand in here and hold the top closed so we don't have to smell it."

Sandy did as Cam instructed and watched her pop a capsule of Benadryl out of the package. She grabbed a bottle

57

of water and twisted the top off. "Let me hold your bag while you take this," she said as she took the bag in one hand and gave Sandy the capsule with the other. "Okay, that's good. Let's go find the hotel and get settled in. That pill may make you sleepy."

"I'm sorry I ruined your day, Cam."

"You didn't ruin it, Squirt. As long as I'm with you, it's a great day."

Cam walked around the Jeep, climbed back in, then located the hotel they were booked into for the night. She took the bag of vinegar and gave Sandy paper towels to dry her arm as she emptied the foul-smelling liquid onto the ground. "I'll be right back." Cam went inside, paid for the room, and walked back to the Jeep. She pulled into the parking spot in front of the room and carried Sandy inside, where she placed her on the bed and handed her the remote. "You hang tight while I unload the Jeep."

"Can I at least rinse my arm?"

"Yes, but right back onto the bed with you."

"Yes, Mama," she teased.

Cam carried in their bags and supplies, then pulled the top up on the Jeep. It didn't look like rain, but it could come up quick on a barrier island. When she walked back into the room, Sandy's eyes were growing heavy as she tried to concentrate on the television.

She looked up at Cam and gave her a goofy smile. "Will you come lie down with me?"

Cam kicked off her shoes and climbed into the bed beside her, careful not to brush against Sandy's wrist. "How are you feeling?"

"Sleepy, but the sting isn't too bad."

"Go ahead and take a nap, and when you wake up we'll put some cream on it."

"Okay, Cam."

She snuggled into Cam, and placed her head on her shoulder and draped her injured wrist across Cam's stomach. Cam wrapped an arm around her and rubbed her back until Sandy drifted off to sleep. Her eyes grew heavy in the dark room as she tried to focus on the TV, and she soon felt herself nodding off.

†

Sandy twitching in her sleep woke Cam three hours later. Her eyes adjusted to the dark and she glanced at the bedside alarm clock to find it was almost eight in the evening. *Damn, I hadn't planned on that.* Sandy was still snuggled into her side, and Cam contemplated waking her to eat or if she should let her sleep. Sandy must have sensed Cam's movement and her eyes fluttered open.

"Hey, Squirt, how're ya feeling?"

Sandy smiled. "Better. Did I sleep long?"

"We both slept for three hours. I reckon we were tired. Are you hungry?"

Sandy nodded. "A little bit."

"Do you feel like going out to eat?"

"I wouldn't mind having a few more mater sandwiches with you, but if you want to go out, we can. This is your trip."

Cam was quick to correct her. "Nope, this is our trip. I'm good with mater sandwiches too." She climbed from the bed. "Do you want to put your pajamas on while I make the sandwiches?" She turned on the bedside light. "Let me look at your wrist."

Sandy held out her arm, and Cam inspected it closely. The welt had turned an angry red while they slept. "Is it itching yet?"

59

"It wasn't until you asked," Sandy said and ran her fingers lightly over the welt.

"Let's put some of the anti-itch cream on it."

Cam opened the box and pulled out the tube, then placed a liberal amount over the welted skin. "Does it hurt to touch it?"

"Not really, but it makes it itch."

"Hopefully this will help." She placed the tube next to the bed. "Go ahead and get changed and I'll fix supper."

"I think I'll rinse my legs off too. They still feel salty."

"You want to take a shower?"

"No, I'll just rinse my legs."

"Okay, Squirt. Holler if you need my help."

"I will. Thanks, Cam."

Cam walked into the small kitchenette area and pulled out the container of tomato slices, the bottle of mayo, and a cold bottle of water. She made another pile of sandwiches while listening for Sandy. She was adding chips to their plates when Sandy exited the bathroom wearing a faded LSU T-shirt and a pair of purple gym shorts.

"I reckon I'll have to get you some new T-shirts when I hit campus."

"I'd like that, Cam. Do you think I can get one with your jersey number on it?"

"Now that, I don't know, but it won't hurt to try. Maybe a football jersey."

"That would work too." She grinned.

"I'll see what I can do. Climb on up and let's eat."

✝

After they finished eating, Cam propped Sandy up on some pillows on the bed. "I'm going to shower and get ready for bed. See if you can find something on TV."

Cam heard Sandy scrolling through the channels as she stripped and stepped under the flow of water. Cam bathed, and when she reached for the towel to dry her body, she heard a familiar sound. She pulled on a T-shirt and shorts and took a running leap onto the bed. "Godzilla, look out," she called as she landed beside Sandy.

"*Godzilla versus Mothra*." Sandy grinned. "Not the new version, one of the originals."

"Man, I love those," Cam laughed.

"So fake I can even see through them."

"Well, they were made long before you or I were born, so they are pretty old. But you have to admit the new ones aren't half as good."

"Or half as funny." She giggled.

"True dat." Cam put her arm around Sandy and they snuggled as Godzilla defended Tokyo from Mothra. They both startled during the fight scenes and laughed at the subtitles that didn't match the movements of the actors' mouths.

"This is way too funny," Sandy giggled.

When the movie ended, Cam asked, "What should we do tomorrow?"

"What do you want to do, Cam?"

"Let's ride around the island for a bit, and if we don't see anything of interest, we'll start back and stop in Nawlins if you want."

"That sounds good to me."

"Maybe we can stop off for beignets and hit the French Market before all the hungover people wake up."

"I love beignets."

"Let's call it a night so we can get up early and hit the road."

CHAPTER SIX

They were awake, showered, and on the road by six. Cam had loaded their bags and dropped the top on the Jeep. They drove a circuit around the island. Cam remembered visiting when she was about Sandy's age and was disappointed to see how touristy it had become and was ready to turn back north.

"Are you ready to go to Nawlins?"

"Let's do it." Sandy grinned.

Cam watched Sandy's hair blowing in the wind as they rode north. "You cold?"

"A little chilly, but it'll warm up soon."

"I can turn some heat on if we need to."

"Nope, I'm good."

As they crossed the river back into New Orleans, she noticed Sandy rubbing her wrist.

"You need some cream?"

"Yes, it's starting to itch."

"It's in the glove box. Can you get it, or do you need my help?"

"I've got this, Cam."

Cam was worried the welt would leave a scar on Sandy's wrist. Not the kind of souvenir she wanted her to take home with her. Hopefully they'd find something at the French Market. Traffic was still light as she turned toward Jackson Square, and their luck held out and she found a parking spot close to the French Market. They secured the Jeep and crossed over to get beignets for breakfast.

Sandy found them a table while Cam placed their order. She carried a large milk for Sandy and a steaming cup of chicory coffee to the table. Several minutes later, a server brought them a bag of the powdered-sugar–coated pastries.

"Careful, they still may be hot," Cam warned as she tore open the bag.

"Where's your order?"

"You think you can eat all of these?"

"Probably so; I'm hungry."

"All right, hotshot, go for it," Cam said and took one of the fried delicacies and bit into it. "You eat the rest and I'll buy more."

Sandy picked up a beignet, and when she bit into it, the white powdered sugar flew everywhere and covered her entire lower face.

"Ha, you look like a ghost," Cam teased.

Sandy used a napkin to wipe across her face, smearing more than she removed. Cam let her eat, knowing there would be plenty more caked on her face before Sandy was full. After they finished, they'd go to the washroom to clean up. She chewed slowly and sipped her coffee while Sandy finished a beignet and plucked another from the bag.

Sandy hit a wall about halfway through the next and dropped the sugary treat on her napkin to take a sip of milk. "Hmmm, three left," Cam grinned and said as she looked into the bag. "You're not done, are you?"

"I'll be doing good to finish this one, Cam," she admitted. "I forgot how big they are."

"I think I may be able to handle one more. Should we take the other two and let your sisters fight over them?"

"Or we could eat them on our way home to prevent a fight, and destroy the evidence."

"You are way too smart, but I do love the way you think. You may have to change shirts, though." She pointed to Sandy's shirt and bit into her beignet.

Sandy looked down at her shirt, covered with the powdered sugar. "Well dang."

"No worries, we'll blow it out on the way home. Finish up and we'll hit the washroom to get some of this sugar off our faces."

She struggled, but Sandy finished the second beignet and her milk. "I'm stuffed."

"You did well." Cam popped the last bite into her mouth. She rolled down the top of the bag and picked up her coffee. "Let's get cleaned up."

It took them several minutes, but when they emerged from the bathroom, their faces were sugar-free and Sandy's shirt held only a faint sign of the white powder.

"Let's hit the French Market," Cam said and reached for Sandy's hand.

They strolled through the vendor stalls, and Sandy rushed over to a rack of aprons. "This would look good on Mama," she said as she picked out one with a red crawfish holding a spatula on the front.

"Yes, it would," she agreed and pulled out money for Sandy to make the purchase. "I think Dad may like one of these pocketknives too," Cam said and handed her more money.

Cam watched her make the purchase, then looked to her left and spotted a stack of T-shirts. They were red with the word *Trouble* in white on the chest, and each had a single number from one through six. She held up two shirts. "How about these for us, Trouble One and Trouble Two?"

"That's us for sure," she giggled.

They paid for their shirts, then slipped into the restroom to change into them. When they emerged, Sandy slid her hand back into Cam's and smiled at her.

They spent the rest of the morning walking around Jackson Square, then walked back to the Jeep to start for home.

"You getting hungry? I am," Cam asked.

"I could eat."

"How about a po boy before we hit the road?"

"Sounds good to me, but can we split one?"

"Of course we can. Is your belly still full of beignets?"

"A little bit, but I am hungry."

Cam ordered a shrimp po boy and a large Coke and they sat at a picnic table to enjoy the meal.

"Man this is good," she said as she popped a shrimp in her mouth.

"Yes, it is," Sandy agreed.

Cam noticed her scratching at her wrist. "Is it time for more itch cream?"

"Yeah, it's starting to burn again."

"Why don't you take another Benadryl too? That may help."

"I don't want to go to sleep. I want to enjoy every minute with you I can."

Cam's heart lodged in her throat at Sandy's emotional plea. "Okay, no Benadryl, but just remember we have it if the cream doesn't work."

"Okay, Cam."

Sandy spread the cream on her wrist while Cam placed the bags in the backseat. "Mama's gonna love that apron."

"I think so too."

Cam rolled the top back on the Jeep and secured it before climbing inside. She grinned at Sandy. "Let's go home."

They pulled on their shades and drove north, the afternoon sun burning down on them. When Cam pulled off the interstate, she glanced over to find Sandy napping. It was a short trip, but she had really enjoyed spending the time with her. She smiled at the memory of Sandy slipping into the shirt, her chest puffing out with pride to be wearing the same shirt as her big sister and she knew it would hold a treasured memory for them both for years to come.

When they were five minutes from home, Cam reached over to gently shake her awake. "Time to wake up, Squirt. We're almost there."

Sandy stretched. "Already?"

"Yes'm," she answered, then stopped on the side of a bridge as the sun went down. "I want to thank you for going with me and sharing this adventure." She pointed at the setting sun. "Just like the sunset, this one is done, but there will be many more for us to share."

Sandy looked up at Cam, tears welling in her eyes that were no longer protected by sunglasses. "I love you, Cam."

"Love you too, Squirt. I wonder what Mama's cooking for supper."

"Are you hungry again?"

"Well yeah, driving's hard work." She winked and pulled back onto the road.

†

Cam stayed busy helping her dad, and the time came for her to leave home for college. She had met Bren for lunch the previous day. Bren seemed happy and appeared to be enjoying her job at LB's.

She reached over and covered Cam's hand with her own. "I'm going to miss spending time with you, but I realize we both have different paths to follow. You have been my best friend forever, and I love you, Cam."

"I love you too, and I hope Rudy knows what a great woman he's about to marry."

"I don't think anyone understands me the way you do, Cam. You probably thought you were the only one with a schoolgirl crush, but I have always loved you. Different from what I feel for Rudy, but love just the same."

Tears filled Cam's eyes. Bren had never confessed an attraction to her before, and it seemed almost cruel she would do it now, the day before Cam left for college. She forced back her tears. "I hope he'll make you happy."

"If not, I'm gonna threaten him with you and Sandy."

Cam laughed, breaking the sudden tension. "Sandy will put a whooping on him."

When it was time for her to return to work, Bren tightly hugged Cam. "Be good to yourself and have fun. You'll grow up all too soon."

"Yes, Mama," Cam teased.

"I'd better not hear of you being in town without coming by to see me either," Bren warned.

"I'll keep that in mind. I'll be seeing you, Bren."

†

During the three-day orientation for new students, Cam would get her class schedules, settle into her new home, and become familiar with the campus. She and Tab had talked several times over the summer, and Tab planned to meet her at the apartment they would share. When her Jeep was packed, she hugged her sisters and her parents.

"I'm going to miss you all."

"You'll be back soon. So go, and have a good time," Ronny said.

Sandy couldn't hold back her tears, breaking Cam's heart. She knelt and hugged her close. "Remember what I said about the sunset," she whispered. "Our adventures are just beginning."

Sandy sniffled and nodded as she brushed back the tears. "I know, Cam."

"I'll see you soon." Cam knew she needed to get on the road before she started crying, so she climbed into the Jeep. She waved and watched in the mirror as she drove away. They all waved back, except for Sandy who clung to her dad's leg.

Damn, I didn't think it would be this hard to leave. Tears rolled down her cheeks as her family disappeared and she headed for Baton Rouge.

CHAPTER SEVEN

Tab was sitting on the front porch of the apartment complex assigned to the female athletes, waiting for Cam to arrive. She was excited to welcome her new teammate to campus and to start her orientation. They would start fall workouts in a week, so she wanted to show Cam as much fun as possible. Cam attended a brief orientation class in the morning, then Tab would walk her through registering for classes and purchasing her books and other supplies.

The team would meet up on Saturday night at a party spot on the river to welcome the new players. They had five freshmen and a transfer from a junior college in Pensacola who they had to welcome to campus and the team. Tab and the two other upper-class team captains were responsible for making sure everyone stayed out of trouble, but had a good time and an opportunity to begin the bonding process.

Her smile grew when a black Jeep pulled into a parking spot and Cam stepped out. Cam looked up and returned her smile.

"Welcome to Baton Rouge, my friend," Tab said as she hugged Cam.

"Thanks, it's great to finally be here."

"Let's get you unloaded and settled in."

They carried a load of boxes inside and Tab hollered out to their neighbors. "Yo, Ruth and Liz, how about some help here."

Two women stepped out into the hall from their apartment and Tab introduced them as Liz Walker, first baseman, and Ruth Sasser, catcher.

"I'm so glad to meet y'all, and thanks for the help."

"No problem. Welcome to LSU," Ruth said and shared one of her infectious smiles with Cam.

They were carrying the last of the boxes in when a pickup truck pulled up.

"Hey, Bugsy," Cam called when she walked past it.

"What's up, Cam?"

"Just getting settled into my apartment. Let me drop this load and I'll come back to help you."

"We all will." Tab grinned. "I think you're rooming with Lori Winters."

"That's right," Bugsy answered. "I wasn't lucky enough to get a room with Cam." She grinned at Tab. The sarcasm in her voice was obvious.

Tab let the comment slide and smiled at her.

"I saw her headed upstairs a few minutes ago," Liz said. "I'll holler at her, and she can help too."

✝

Once everyone settled in, Tab asked Cam, "You ready to try out cafeteria food?"

"Yeah, I think I've worked up an appetite."

"Don't get too excited. It's definitely not your mama's cooking, but it's decent and there's plenty of everything."

As they stepped into the hallway, they found Liz and Ruth were also heading out to eat. "Time to grub?" Liz asked.

"Yep, we might as well break her in right," Tab teased.

It wasn't a fancy place, but the food was better than she imagined, based on Tab's comments. "Is there always this many choices?" Cam asked.

Tab smiled and took a seat across from her. "Usually there's always a lot of protein, and plenty choices of vegetables."

"Right up my alley," Cam said, then bit into a piece of chicken. "Yes'm, yard bird, and country groceries."

"Eat up, country girl."

†

As they walked back to the apartments, Tab leaned over to Cam. "Is there something between you and Bugsy? Her comment today seemed off."

"Bugsy has been hitting on me for years and just won't take no for an answer. She was hoping we'd be roomies."

"Too bad, I snatched you up before she could. Do you think she's going to be a problem for you, playing on the same team?"

"No, I'm used to Bugsy's antics, but thank you."

Tab bumped her with a shoulder. "No problem. That's what roomies are for."

†

She and Tab sat up talking until nearly midnight.

71

"We'd better hit the sack. You've got orientation at nine. Would you like to grab some breakfast and I'll show you where you need to go?"

"That sounds great. Thanks for all your help. This place is much bigger than I dreamed."

"You'll get used to it before long. I'll meet you after orientation and we'll get you signed up for classes. We can get your books and other supplies tomorrow."

Cam disappeared into the bathroom to wash her face and brush her teeth. When she returned, Tab had changed into a long T-shirt.

"Are you an early riser?" Tab asked from the bathroom.

"Usually, yes," Cam answered. "Are you?"

"I'm normally up and drinking coffee by six."

"That's good. I'm noisy in the morning."

"Do you sing in the shower?"

"Umm, sometimes," Cam confessed.

Tab chuckled. "Go for it."

Cam slipped into her nightclothes, and climbed into the bed. She was surprised at how comfortable it was.

"Are you ready for lights-out?" Tab asked.

"Yeah, I am."

"Good night, John Boy," Tab said.

"Good night, Mary Ellen," Cam answered with a laugh.

Cam was afraid her excitement would keep her awake, but she drifted to sleep minutes after lying down.

✝

Cam was relieved that orientation went well, and by Friday afternoon she was registered for school, had purchased the books and supplies she needed, and was confident she could find all her classes. She had registered her Jeep with the university and purchased a parking permit.

She could legally drive her Jeep, but the time finding a parking space would take wasn't worth the trouble. Walking was her best option, and it would help to keep her legs in shape.

†

After dinner Friday night, Cam and Tab were walking back to the apartment when they heard loud honking of horns and turned to see a line of RVs heading toward the football stadium.

"Let the insanity begin," Tab chuckled. "RVs have been arriving since Thursday as fans pour in to tail-gate in anticipation for the first home game of the year. Thursday through Sunday afternoon will remain crazy as a bunch of Cajuns descend on campus."

"Do we get tickets to the games?"

Tab nudged her with a shoulder. "Oh, heck yeah, li'l sister."

"Is it hard to get extras, like if I had family visit who wanted to go?"

"It's usually not too bad. We're close enough to the stadium that some of the team just stays home and parties while the open windows give us the play-by-play. No fighting the traffic or the masses of people leaving Death Valley."

"So what do you do on a Friday night on campus?"

"We play some pickup ball usually, basketball or volleyball, or play cards and drink beer."

"Does Coach do any pop-in checks?"

"Sometimes, but mostly during the off-season. She trusts us to be college students and have some fun. She demands the upperclassmen keep an eye on the team's behavior, to

73

ensure things don't get out of hand. After the new year, you can forget beer for the next six months."

"Coach seems pretty cool."

"She is, but she'll work you harder and expect more out of you than ever before in your life." Tab smiled and held up her right hand, measuring an inch between her thumb and forefinger. "We were this close to going to the College World Series last year, but fell short in the SEC tournament. She's got hopes that with you and the other rookies coming in, it will provide that extra talent to get us a ride to Oklahoma City."

"No pressure there." Cam grinned.

"We have a good team, but we had some weak spots that needed to be plugged. You gonna do dat, roomie." Tab chuckled.

"Do we get extra time in the batting cages in the fall?"

"Nope, it's mostly physical conditioning until nearly the end of the semester, when she'll let us start hitting."

"Dang, I'm used to hitting all year round when I can."

"Coach is adamant about it. She doesn't want anyone to burn out by starting too early. She teases us that she wants us to save all the good swings for the games." Tab's eyes sparkled with excitement when she talked about Coach or the team.

"So what's it going to be tonight?"

"From the sound of it, I'd say they are already on the volleyball court," Tab said as they walked around the side of the apartment complex.

"It's about time you two got here," Ruth groaned. "They're kicking our butts."

"Have no fear, T and C are here," Tab called back.

"T and C, huh? Best you could come up with?" Ruth chuckled.

"On short notice, yes."

"What about the dynamic duo, or terrifying twosome?" Cam suggested.

"You gotta earn those titles first," Ruth hollered, "so get your butts in here."

Cam shook her head. "We gotta work on your nickname skills."

"Whatever, killer," Tab teased.

The games were all in good fun, but the softball players didn't stand a chance against the taller, more experienced volleyball team.

"Good games, ladies. We can't wait to get you out on the diamond," Tab hollered as they left the court after losing three straight games. "Well, if nothing else, we bolstered their confidence a bit."

Cam laughed. "Hah, yeah right. Umm, no, I don't think so. We were no competition for them at all."

"Maybe we should challenge them to basketball. They'd still have a height advantage, but I got a killer jump shot," Ruth suggested.

"Now you're thinking, Ruth." Tab offered her a high five.

"I've got some cold ones in the fridge if y'all want to come up."

Tab looked at Cam. "Sounds good to me. You game?"

"I'm right there with ya."

†

"I'm making some nachos, if you want to grab some beers, honey," Liz said as they entered. Ruth smacked Liz on the butt as she walked past, then gave her a beer and a quick kiss on her way back through the kitchen.

Tab watched Cam closely to see how she reacted to the public display of affection. She was sure Cam had witnessed the full interaction, but she showed no sign of repulsed or embarrassed by Ruth and Liz's behavior. She smiled to herself. *Maybe, just maybe.*

"Is there anything I can help you with?"

"Thanks, Cam, but this kitchen isn't big enough for two. Better grab a seat on the couch before these two hog it." Liz nodded toward Tab and Ruth.

"Come on." Tab held out her hand and led Cam to a small couch.

After they settled around a coffee table, Liz smiled at Cam. "So tell us about yourself, rookie."

"What do you want to know?"

"Everything. You got a boyfriend or girlfriend? What do you plan to major in? Boxers, bikinis, or briefs?" Liz teased.

"No, no; I don't know; and boxers or bikinis." She grinned.

"So no steady back home?" Ruth said, and shot a look at Tab.

"No, I was crushing on my best friend for years, but it was just a schoolgirl crush. She's getting married next Valentine's, so I concentrated on playing ball and getting out of high school."

"That's cool," Liz said. "It took me about six months to convince Ruth I was the one for her."

Cam smiled at Ruth. "Slow learner?"

Tab and Liz broke out laughing. "One too many cleats to the head," Tab teased.

"Hey now, I wasn't that bad." She looked at Liz. "Was I?"

"No, baby, we're just teasing you. You started slow, but woman, you have made up for it ever since." She leaned in to kiss Ruth.

They shared the nachos and drank a few beers. Liz placed her bottle on the table and looked at Tab. "Are y'all going to the ball game tomorrow?"

"I don't know." She looked at Cam. "Are we?"

"I've never been inside Death Valley."

"Yes, we're going to the game. Y'all?"

"We are now," Ruth said.

"The game starts at one, so do you want to eat at the cafeteria before we go?" Tab asked.

"Might as well. You know they rob ya blind with the price of food at the stadium," Ruth groaned.

"That's so true. Meet y'all at eleven, then?"

Liz nodded, "Yep, that works for us, Tab."

†

"I'm going to hit the shower and the bed," Tab announced when they returned to their apartment.

Cam closed the window to shut out the noise of the fans already partying at the stadium. "Damn, that's better. I'll shower when you're done, so save me some hot water."

"If you're lucky," Tab said and closed the door behind her.

Cam sat on the small couch and propped her feet on the coffee table after kicking off her shoes. She could hear the shower running in the bathroom and smiled. She had to wonder if her teammates were testing her tonight to see how she would react to their displays of lesbian affection. She hoped she had passed the test by not batting an eye when they had kissed. Just because she hadn't ventured into any type of sexual relationship didn't mean she was totally naïve, and for years, she had harbored a crush on Bren. She'd shocked herself by admitting the crush to her new friends so easily. Playing sports all her life, she had met many girls who

77

had relationships with other girls, and Cam hadn't been scared away from forming friendships by their sexual orientation. She looked around the apartment at the pictures of Tab, but other than family and team photos, she didn't seem to have anyone special of either sex.

Could Tab be gay? Even more importantly, could I? She tried to remember any time in her life that she had shown interest in a boy, and she couldn't remember one. She must have been frowning, because Tab asked, "What's the frown for?"

Cam jumped at the sound of Tab's voice. She had been concentrating so intensely, she hadn't realized Tab had emerged from the bathroom. "Sorry, didn't realize I was frowning. I was just thinking."

Tab tossed the covers back on her bed and sat. "Was it painful?"

"Was what painful?" she asked, then realized Tab was teasing.

"Thinking so hard it made you frown."

"I was just trying to remember something, but I couldn't think of it. It's all good, though."

"You sure we don't need me to take you to the hospital to have you tested for dementia? You're mighty young to have that already."

"No, smartass." Cam shook her head and walked in to the bathroom.

"Good, I hate waiting in emergency rooms."

"You're safe this weekend," Cam said and closed the door behind her.

†

Tab stretched out on her bed with her arms above her head, watching the shadows dance across the ceiling from the candle she'd lit. She was pleased Cam had not been repulsed or run from the room when Liz and Ruth kissed. Her attraction to the rookie was growing rapidly, and she admired the way Cam talked about the loving relationship she had with her family. All her life Tab had wished to have such a close-knit relationship with her parents, but the warmth she felt when Cam talked of her family was nothing like the distant affection she felt from her own. She relaxed watching the shadows. Her eyes grew heavy and she was nearly asleep when Cam emerged from the bathroom.

✝

"You want me to blow out that candle?"

"Sure," Tab answered and stretched lazily.

Cam extinguished the candle before stretching out on her bed. With the window closed, the noise from the stadium disappeared, leaving the room deathly silent. She pulled the covers over her body and rolled onto her side, facing Tab's bed. She couldn't see Tab's face, but she sensed she was still awake. Her pulse raced as she gathered up the nerve to ask Tab the question burning through her veins. Finally she spoke. "Can I ask you a question?"

She sensed that Tab's head had turned toward her. "Of course. You can ask me anything."

"Are you gay?" she blurted out before she lost her nerve.

"Yes, I am. Does that bother you?"

"Nope, not at all. I was just curious, you know, after Liz and Ruth, you know, kissed each other."

"Those two just can't keep their hands off each other, but they are very much in love. They've been together for almost two years and are pretty much inseparable."

Cam heard the affection in Tab's voice. "Are there a lot of lesbians on the team?"

"I've only slept with half of them, so I don't know about the other half."

"What?" Cam cried out.

"I'm teasing, silly. I've only slept with one of our current teammates. I sure would've liked to have seen your face just then, though," she snickered.

"I'm trying to be mature and serious about this and you're being a goof," Cam scolded.

"I'm sorry, I just couldn't resist teasing you a bit. Yes, part of the team has girlfriends, and a few have boyfriends, and I wouldn't be surprised if one or two have both."

"What about you?"

"No, I don't have both."

Cam could imagine Tab's smirk. "Are you being deliberately obtuse?"

"Damn, that's a big word for a freshman."

"Ugh, you're impossible," Cam growled and rolled away from her.

"If you must know, yes, I'm gay, and no, I'm presently unattached, but I'm considering opening up the application process, so if you know of anyone who might be interested, send 'em my way."

"Applications? You are just not right, Fortner. Good night."

"Wait just a minute, you started this conversation."

"Well, on that note, I think Bugsy might be very interested."

"Nope, not gonna happen. She's not my type. Besides, she's too obsessed with you."

"Not your type? What is your type?"

"Not sure. I haven't found her yet."

"Should we skip the game tomorrow and pass out your applications instead? Or posters with a large question mark on them, with a notice for auditions?"

"Hah. I'm so glad I picked you as roomie. You give as good as you take."

Cam smiled. "I'll take that as a compliment. I think," she answered. "Good night, Tab."

"Good night, John Boy," Tab replied, quoting from a favorite show The Walton's.

Cam's mind reeled with the information she had learned about Tab and some of her teammates. She had to admit that other than Bren, Tab was the only other person she had felt attracted to, but she wasn't sure that was enough to make her a lesbian. She couldn't help but think of how soft Tab's lips would feel as she listened to her breathing slow as she drifted off to sleep.

✝

Cam had awoken early and decided to take a run before showering and going for breakfast. When she slipped back into the room as quietly as possible, Tab was sleeping, a peaceful smile playing across her face.

There is no denying she is a handsome woman.

Tab barely twitched as Cam walked into the bathroom to strip and start the shower.

✝

"Shit," Tab whispered when the shower started. Cam had been quiet when she returned from running, but Tab had still woken at the sensation of movement inside the apartment. Now that she was awake, her bladder screamed for relief. She couldn't possibly hold it until Cam finished showering, so she waited until she heard the shower curtain slide into place, then knocked on the door. "Cam, can I come in? I really need to pee."

81

"Yeah, sure, come on in."

Tab sat on the toilet and relieved her aching bladder. She was surprised she could hold that much fluid inside her body. "Ah, thanks," she called out as she finished. "Gonna flush now, so you might wanna step back for a second."

"Thanks for the warning."

Tab pushed the handle and moved to wash her hands. "No problem, I've been blasted a few times when a roomie forgot to warn me."

"I've been meaning to ask you why you didn't already have a roomie."

Tab leaned against the wall as she watched the movement behind the semi-clear shower curtain. "Desi graduated last year. She played on the volleyball team and is now over in Europe somewhere playing professionally."

"Were the two of you more than roomies?"

"My, you are a curious one, aren't you? We were friends with benefits, but never a serious item. We both dated others."

"So you could have picked a new roomie from someone else already here?"

"Of course I could have, but I heard we had a cocky young shortstop coming in that would probably need someone older and wiser to keep her out of trouble."

"So you're taking one for the team. Is that what you're telling me?"

"Yeah, basically you could say that," Tab said and broke out laughing until she realized Cam had turned off the water. Her eyes went wide as Cam's hand pulled back the curtain and her wet, naked body filled her vision.

"Will you toss me a towel?" Cam requested as she squeezed the water from her hair.

Tab had to tear her eyes away from Cam's body to reach for one.

A flush crept up Tab's neck as her eyes devoured Cam's body, and she couldn't help but smile. Cam took the towel Tab offered. "Thanks. I'm going for some breakfast, if you'd like to join me."

"Sure, that sounds good. Let me throw on some sweats." Tab raced out of the bathroom, careful to close the door behind her.

"Damn, that's one smoking-hot body," she whispered to herself. She slipped into a pair of sweatpants and a loose T-shirt, then a pair of flip-flops. Her face was still red and hot. "Lordy, Lordy, I'm doomed."

†

When she pulled the shower curtain back, Cam needed great restraint to keep from breaking out in laughter at the look on Tab's face. She was certain the heat emanating from Tab's face elevated the temperature in the small room as Tab struggled to tear her eyes off Cam's body. If she had any doubt that Tab was interested in more than friendship, those doubts disappeared the moment Tab's eyes devoured her body, and Cam nearly choked on her laughter.

Cam had no idea how to proceed with Tab, so she decided to let Mother Nature lead them into a relationship if that was meant to be. *Hell, who am I kidding? I have no clue how to go about this at all. Tab would have a lot to teach me, if she was up to the task.*

She finished dressing and emerged from the bathroom to find Tab sitting on her own bed. Still slightly flushed, she smiled up at Cam. "You ready to roll?"

"I can eat." She stood and headed for the door.

"Hey, good morning," Tab called out as Liz and Ruth passed. "Going for breakfast?"

83

"Dontcha know it." Ruth placed an arm across Tab's shoulders. "Come on, hotshot."

Cam smiled at the women walking ahead of them, "How ya doing this morning, Liz?"

"Good, thanks, and you?"

"I couldn't be better."

Liz fell back a step to walk with Cam and nodded toward Tab. "She treating you okay?"

"Yeah, she's really cool. Easy on the eyes too," Cam said before realizing what she was doing.

Liz grinned at Cam. "A girl could do much worse for herself. Tab's a good person."

"She was telling me about taking applications for a girlfriend. You think I should apply?"

Liz placed her arm across Cam's shoulder. "You ever had a girlfriend before?"

"Nope, I haven't a clue what to do." Cam slowed down to put some distance between Ruth and Tab, who were walking ahead of them.

"The best advice I could give you is to communicate well. Tell her what you like, and what you need. Tab's got some experience and can help you learn what you want to know."

"That excites me and terrifies me at the same time. Is that normal?"

"I think it's very normal, especially for your first time. There's no need to hurry, so take your time and let nature take its course."

Ruth turned her head and smiled at her lover. "What you two doing back there?"

"Just admiring the fine view," Liz answered with a wink.

Tab turned to find Cam smiling at her. "Not near as good as the view I had this morning."

Cam broke out laughing.

Liz looked at her. "Do tell, rookie."

"She got flashed when I finished showering this morning. I wouldn't have thought anything could make the great Tab Fortner speechless, but she made a pretty quick exit."

"I would have loved to have seen that." Ruth bumped into a furiously blushing Tab.

"Okay, y'all can stop now."

They entered the building and saw Bugsy was also heading to the cafeteria. "Hey, Bugsy," Cam hollered.

"Morning, ladies. Cam." She grinned. "Are y'all going to the game later? I hear we get tickets."

"Dontcha know it. Geaux Tigers!" Liz cheered. "The first game of the season is usually a warm-up for the start of the season, but it'll be guaranteed for a lot of touchdowns."

Ruth gave her lover a high five. "That's always fun to watch."

"We're planning on grabbing some lunch around eleven and then walking to the stadium if you want to join us," Liz offered.

"Thanks, I've barely seen Lori. She comes in after I've gone to bed, so I'm starting to get a complex."

"No worries, it's not you. She's just head over heels for her boyfriend." Ruth rolled her eyes.

Cam caught the dramatic emphasis on the word *boyfriend*. "Does he spend much time at the apartment?"

"No, she spends a lot of time over at his and comes back to sleep at ours. Usually, that is."

Lori must be one of the girls that are strictly dickly. Good Lord, where did that come from? She shook the thought out of her head to keep from laughing.

Tab must have seen the look of amusement on her face and cocked an eyebrow at her, but didn't say anything.

She held the door open for the group and winked at Cam as she walked by.

85

†

After consuming a large portion of the bacon and eggs prepared for the day, the group kicked back to enjoy their coffee.

"Damn, I'm not sure I'll need lunch after eating all that," Cam groaned.

Tab huffed, "Who you kidding? You'll be hollering, 'I'm hungry,' again in three hours."

"Probably so." Cam grinned back at her.

Ruth leaned toward the table. "We still on for the river later tonight?"

"Heck yeah, we got newbies to break in." Tab smirked. "Speaking of which, we need to make a beer run this morning so we can get it on ice."

"I guess that means I'm driving, since the coolers won't fit in your car," Ruth said.

Bugsy's head popped up. "I've got a truck we can use."

"Thanks, but you're going to be busy tonight, and it's my turn to be designated driver," Ruth replied.

"Some of them may be riding in the back on the way home," Liz reminded her lover.

Tab and Cam exchanged a look. "Does that mean we have to cancel any plans for church tomorrow morning?" Cam asked.

"Um, I don't think you'll be up to worshipping anything unless it's the porcelain goddess." Liz grinned.

"So this is our rookie initiation?" Cam asked.

Ruth grinned. "One of them."

Bugsy groaned. "Dare I ask how many there are?"

Liz shrugged. "It varies from class to class."

"Don't worry, we won't let anything get too out of hand, or Coach will kill us," Tab assured them.

"Coach knows about this?" Cam asked.

Ruth nodded. "Yes, she does, and she encourages it for team-building. She remembers what it was like to be a college student, ya know."

"That's cool," Bugsy chimed in. "Will the entire team be there?"

"Most of us, without boyfriends too." Liz winked.

"Hmm, so it's an all-woman affair?" Cam asked.

"Damn, you're right, Fortner, she is a smart one," Ruth said, and punched Cam's shoulder.

†

Cam slid into the bench seat between Ruth and Tab before they went on the beer run.

"Brandy and Max are going out early to set up the fire and make sure no one else has laid claim to our spot," Ruth told Tab.

"I sure hope not. That's the perfect spot for our group."

"That it is."

Ruth pulled into a local liquor store, and Tab grabbed a cart as they entered.

"Do you think three cases of Coronas and one of Miller Lite will be enough? What about for shots?"

Ruth grinned. "That should be plenty. So how about a liter of Fireball?"

"I do love the way you think, Sasser." Tab grinned and pulled out a credit card. "Will you grab some of those disposable shot glasses, rookie?"

"Sure thing, boss," Cam replied.

Tab looked at Ruth. "See. Smart, just like I told ya."

"I'm glad you approve," Cam said as she dropped the plastic glasses in the cart.

"Add six bags of ice too, please."

"Woohoo, someone's having a party," the cashier said as she scanned the contents of the cart. "Is this an open party?" she asked, smiling sweetly at Tab.

"Sorry, sweets, private this time," she answered and shot the young woman a wink.

"Have fun, then. See you next time," she said as she handed the card back to Tab. "Sign here, please."

Tab signed the receipt and tucked her wallet in her pocket. Cam pushed the cart as they exited the store. "Can I offer to pay for some of this?" she asked as they stopped in front of the ice machine.

Tab smiled. "You could, but I'd just tell you thanks but no. My parents are both lawyers and expect me to have a great time while doing my undergrad work. My spending budget is unlimited as long as my grades are high."

"Then off to law school to follow in their footsteps?"

"More than likely, especially if they get their way."

"What do you want to do? Is that given any consideration?"

"To be honest, I think it's been planned since preschool." Tab chuckled, but Cam heard a hint of sadness in her voice. "So I'm going to enjoy myself for my last two years, then it's buckle-down time."

As if sensing a change in topic was needed, Ruth asked, "Are you leaning toward any particular major, Cam?"

"I've really got no clue yet. I figured I'd have at least this year to decide."

"Yep, no need to rush." She climbed into the back of her truck and popped open the lids on two coolers. "Let's load 'em up."

Tab and Cam tore the cases of beer open and handed them to Ruth, then Tab covered them with ice. Ruth closed her bed cover to protect the coolers from the burning sun and prying eyes. The bottle of Fireball joined them in the cab of the truck.

"We've got time to shower and dress for the game," Tab said as she climbed in behind Cam.

"What's the norm for dressing for a game?"

"Just about anything goes," Ruth answered. "It's going to be hot, so I'm wearing some bermuda shorts and a LSU softball polo."

"Sounds cool. I reckon I'll go in shorts and a LSU tee."

"Nope, your awesome roomie has got you hooked up with a brand-new polo of your own." Tab grinned. "The rest will have to wait until tonight, but you're lucky you have connections."

"Wow, thanks, Tab."

She ruffled Cam's hair. "My pleasure, roomie."

†

Tab was right, Cam was hungry by the time they had dressed. She loaded her plate with a bacon cheeseburger and a huge salad. "That should hold me for a while," she told Tab as she sat across from her.

When they emerged from the cafeteria, they could hear the crowd's noise coming from the stadium. She looked at Tab.

"Warm-ups," Tab said. "That and the rowdy crowd tail-gating in the parking lot."

Cam nodded. "It sounds like they are having a good time."

"This is LSU, baby. We always have a good time," she crowed. "Dontcha know we live for football around here?"

Cam smacked her forehead. "How on earth could I forget?"

As they walked to the stadium, the aroma of a variety of foods cooking assaulted her senses. The spicy smells of gumbo, crawfish, and wings mingled with ribs, gator, and a plethora of other meats. It made Cam long for home and the cookouts her family had, especially on football weekends as they watched the game on TV or listened to it on the radio. She could imagine her family scurrying around as they prepared a feast, and she knew Sandy would be stuck to her dad like glue. She needed to give them a call after the game to check in and let them know she was settling in well.

They walked to the booth, showed their student athlete IDs, and received their passes. Cam looked down at the ticket in her hand. "Wow, this is a great seat. I assumed we'd be in the end zone with the rest of the students."

"We are highly encouraged to attend and support all sports teams, so they give us great tickets," Ruth explained. "We can't sell them, but we can share with teammates when family members want to attend."

"That's great. My baby sister is dying to come to a game."

Tab smiled. "That won't be a problem. We can easily get her a ticket."

Cam nodded, and noticed as they walked to their seats that other athletes were also in the section. Volleyball, basketball, track, baseball, and gymnastics all had sections in the stadium. She felt many sets of curious eyes following her as she made her way to her seat. *Fresh meat, I reckon.* She couldn't help but grin at the thought.

†

As predicted, the game wasn't close, but the Tiger offense got a great workout and by the end of the third quarter, second- and third-string players were getting playing time. She had to smile as Tab leaned forward in her seat to watch the players run a tightrope down the sidelines or dive to make a catch. Several times, Tab had grabbed Cam's arm or leg in her excitement, probably without even realizing what she was doing. Liz was sitting on Cam's opposite side, and she leaned in after Tab had grabbed Cam after the Tigers scored a touchdown.

"I should have warned you that you may come out bruised or battered when you sit beside Tab. She really gets into the action."

Cam leaned over to Liz. "I can tell. It's all good, though."

Tab turned to see them watching her. "What?"

"Nothing," Liz answered. "Are we staying for the whole game?"

Tab looked at the scoreboard. With only six minutes left in the game, fans from the opposing team were fleeing the stadium, with hopes of getting a jump on traffic. Interstates and roads leading out of town would be bottlenecked for miles as they made for home.

"Naw, I think we can head out now."

†

The game ended as they made their way from the stadium.

"What time do we need to head out to the river?" Cam asked Tab. "I need to call home."

"Probably in about an hour. Liz, and Ruth will round up the rookies and join the others already out there. You might want to change into some sweats." She grinned. "You can ride out with me."

"But you're not the DD."

"Nope, but I won't drink more than two, so I'll be safe to drive."

91

"Okay. I'm not much of a drinker, if you change your mind. I can always drive you home."

"Thanks, but I won't change. I've got to keep everyone safe."

"You make a good mama."

"Hah. Just wait until you feel the wrath of Coach."

Cam grimaced. "Is she really that bad? She seems so nice."

"Until you get that temper of hers riled up, then you better look out."

"I'll do my best to stay on her good side."

"Smart move, rookie. I'm gonna help Ruth and Liz. I'll see you in a bit."

†

Cam caught a glimpse of her image in the mirror. "Damn, you look sharp," she giggled. She kicked off her shoes, and stripped out of her shirt and shorts. She pulled on her favorite sweatpants and a long-sleeve T-shirt, then sat on the couch and dialed home. The phone rang ten times with no answer, so she hung up and walked to the bathroom to brush her teeth and wash her face. She spritzed her wrist with a perfume and rubbed them together. She'd try calling home again before they left. Cam took out her favorite LSU ball cap and pulled it on.

There, I'm totally casual now, perfect for a campfire and a couple of beers.

She was putting her tennis shoes back on when her stomach grumbled. "No, you cannot be hungry again." Her stomach responded by growling louder. "Okay, it won't be a bad thing to eat something before I drink anyhow." She picked up the phone and dialed home. This time she was pleased when T answered.

"Geaux Tigers, St. Angelo residence."

"Hey, T, it's me, Cam."

Sandy was squealing in the background as Cam tried to answer T's questions. "Yeah, it was a good game. The stadium was rocking for sure. ... Yes, I'm all set to start classes on Monday. ... Heck yeah, I'm nervous. This place is huge. ... Okay, let me talk to Mama, and then I'll talk with Sandy."

Sandy griped in the background about having to wait because Cam wanted to talk with her mama.

"Hey, Mama. ... Yes, ma'am, I'm doing fine. The food's good, but nothing like yours." Cam could sense her mama smiling. "Is everything going well there? ... Yeah, I miss her too. I'll call again later this week. ... Yes, please put her on. ... Love you too, Mama. Tell Dad hello and I love him too."

"Finally," Sandy cried out.

"Hey, Squirt. ... Yeah, I miss you too. ... Yes, it was a great game. ... No, I start school Monday. How are your classes going? ... That sounds good. Are you helping dad out when you get home? It'll be a few weeks before I come home."

The lock on the door clicked and Tab entered the apartment. She smiled at Cam and walked into the bathroom. When she returned, Cam had stretched out on the couch.

"Yes, I got to see Mike. He's a real tiger and has his own little resort here. ... Heck no, I didn't try to pet him." She chuckled. "No, I need both my hands to play ball and to fish."

It was obvious to Tab that Cam was talking with her baby sister Sandy. Tab smiled at her and mouthed the word *aww* before she began changing. The smile plastered on Cam's face was adorable and left no doubt how much she loved her little sister. She tried to be quiet to allow Cam to enjoy her call and changed clothes while she waited.

"Okay, Squirt, I need to get going. ... Love you too and will see you soon. ... Yes, I'll work on getting a ticket for you to come to a game. I'll call Wednesday, okay? Love you." Cam hung up and turned toward Tab, still smiling.

"Everything okay at home?"

"Yes, Sandy said everything was going good. I actually got to talk to Mama a minute before Sandy took over."

"She loves you dearly from the sound of it."

"She's just like me when I was eight."

"Can you go get her next weekend? She can use my ticket to the game and stay here with us."

"I reckon I could. You sure you wouldn't mind her staying?"

"Not if she's just like you. It'll give me some insight into you. I'll even drive you. I only have one class that day and it's at eight in the morning, so we could drive down afterward."

"That would be cool. I have a class at eight too. I could show you around my little home town."

"I'd like that, but I hope this means you're going to have to go home to Monroe with me for a weekend."

"You've got a deal. I'll call them tomorrow and set it up. Thanks, Tab."

"You're welcome. You ready to ride?"

"Yeah, but can we go through a drive-through somewhere? My stomach's growling and I probably need something on it before I drink anything."

"That's not a bad idea. You like chicken fingers?"

"Is the Pope Catholic?"

Tab smiled. "I know just the place, and it's on the way."

✝

When they walked out to the parking lot, Tab pushed the button on a key fob and unlocked the doors on a sleek black convertible Mustang. To say it was beautiful would have been an insult.

"This is yours?"

"Yes, it is. Do you like?"

"Oh hell yes, it's gorgeous."

"Hop in and let's ride. You mind the top down?"

"I prefer it actually."

Tab slid in behind the wheel and pressed a button and the top began retracting. She turned the key in the ignition and the motor roared to life, then settled into a deep purr. The car reeked of power and speed.

They pulled into the parking lot of the restaurant and Tab looked at the line at the drive-through. "We might as well go inside. It'll probably be faster."

"That's fine with me."

After devouring a quick meal, they left. Tab grinned at Cam and tossed her the keys.

"You're really going to let me drive her?"

"No, I'm just teasing. Toss 'em back."

"Hell no." Cam smiled back at her.

†

The spot on the river was twenty minutes from campus, and Cam was delighted to find that Tab knew a route that would prevent them from having to travel any of the roads packed with fans attempting to leave Baton Rouge. The car handled perfectly and Cam fell in love with the Mustang. *Still wouldn't trade my Jeep, but man the power is awesome.*

Cam slowed when Tab pointed out a narrow dirt path. "You want me to drive down that, in this car?"

"Yeah, just take it slow. It opens up once you clear the highway."

Cam heard whooping and hollering ahead of them and saw the glow of the fire as night had fully fallen around them. She pulled to a stop beside Ruth's truck. "Do you want the top up or down?"

"I think it's safe to leave it down."

Cam turned off the car and handed Tab the keys. "Thanks for letting me drive. She's a great car."

"You're welcome. She's a fantastic drive. Let's go have some fun."

✝

Downed trees and beach chairs circled the bright campfire. Cam recognized a few of the team from a recruiting visit, and Tab introduced her to the ones she didn't know. She and Bugsy were two of the five rookies. The transfer from Florida drew her attention immediately as she looked familiar. When Tab introduced her to Parker Lewis, the woman looked up at Cam from her seat. She was attractive with nearly jet-black hair, and green eyes that sparkled when she smiled. She held out her hand to Cam. Cam took it and felt the warm, soft skin close around hers.

"I'm glad we're finally on the same team, St. Angelo. You took me yard twice with your deep home runs in a tournament several years ago when I was still in high school."

Cam smirked. "I thought you looked familiar. I'm looking forward to playing ball with you."

Ruth walked up beside her and handed Tab and Cam a beer.

"Glad you two finally made it," she teased.

"You know we had to stop to feed the bottomless pit," Tab said as she tapped her bottle to Cam's bottle.

Cam tipped her beer to Ruth. "Thanks, Ruth. Did everyone make it out safely?"

"Yes, so far so good. Now I just have to get everyone home safely." She nodded toward Bugsy and another of the new players, Alecia. "I'm not too sure how long those two will make it. Don't seem to be big drinkers."

"The Fireball shots will probably finish them off," Tab said. "I'm gonna go mingle a bit. Have fun."

Cam sat beside Parker and watched as Tab made her rounds speaking to new and old members of the team. She marveled at how confident and comfortable Tab was with talking with people. She was going to make an excellent lawyer one day. She sure could work a crowd.

"Are you two together?" Parker asked.

"As in a couple? No, why do you ask?"

"You'd make a handsome couple, and neither of you can keep your eyes off the other," Parker pointed out. Cam realized she'd been watching Tab, and Parker had caught her in the act. She didn't realize how transparent her attraction had become.

She laughed, and the sound drew Tab's attention. Tab caught her eye and smiled.

"She doesn't smile like that at anyone else in this crowd," Parker said.

A blush rose to Cam's face. "I've never had a girlfriend."

"You haven't? You sure are missing out on a lot of fun, then," Parker said and drained her beer. "I need a new one. Be right back," she added and left Cam contemplating her comments.

Bugsy's laughter filled the air after she finished chugging the remainder of a beer and held on to the bottle. One of her seasoned teammates handed her a fresh one.

97

Someone's going to be hurting in the morning. I've got to remember to pace myself.

Parker returned and sat beside her. "She's going to regret chugging tomorrow."

"I was thinking the same thing. Bugsy's trying too hard to fit in."

"You know her well?"

"We've competed against each other in every sport imaginable since high school."

"Did you go the same school?"

"No, Bugsy is from Opelousas, and I'm from the big city of Morganza."

"Sorry, but I've never heard of either of them."

"They both are very small towns, so that's not surprising. Where are you from?"

"Pensacola, or as most of the locals claim, lower Alabama." Parker chuckled. "A quaint little town on the Gulf."

"I've been through there before. It looks very nice."

"What about your tall drink of water over there?" She nodded toward Tab.

Cam smiled at her comment. "She's from Monroe, several hours north of here."

"I'm majoring in sport psychology. Have you declared a major yet?"

"Nope, I don't even have a clue." Cam shrugged.

"It'll come to you, so don't sweat it. You can major in home runs this year."

"I have to make the starting lineup first," Cam smiled as she reminded her.

"Seriously, like there is any doubt of that. It may not be shortstop, but you can guarantee you'll be in the infield somewhere."

"I hope so. The position doesn't matter much as long as I'm playing. I can do most anything but pitch or catch."

"I pitch and play some third when needed. It looks like we've got plenty of pitchers, so maybe I'll be in the infield with you and do some relief pitching."

"That sounds like a good plan. Well, I guess I should quit being a wallflower and go mingle. Nice to meet you, Parker."

"The pleasure was all mine, ma'am." Parker grinned.

†

Cam spent the next hour talking to her other teammates and drank two more beers, surprising herself by exceeding her limit. The food and drinking slowly helped ward off the effects of the alcohol. She wasn't even feeling buzzed. She noticed a path leading toward the river and decided to take a walk. Cam made her way to the edge of the Mississippi and sat on a log as she watched the blinking lights of barges slowly creeping down the river to New Orleans or other destinations. Mesmerized by how the moon's reflection reminded her of home, she didn't hear Tab walk up beside her until her teammate spoke.

"Relaxing out here, isn't it?"

"Very much so, but it makes me homesick."

"Are you doing okay, John Boy?"

"Maybe a little homesick. This really does remind me of home. You'll understand once you see it."

"That should ease up once classes and practice start up. Are you having a good time tonight?"

"Yes, I am. The rest of the team seems pretty nice."

"I think we've got a decent team. We're about to do the welcoming toast and shot, if you're ready to go. After that, people will start drifting back to campus."

Tab offered her hand and pulled Cam up from her seat.

99

As they walked toward the fire, Cam heard someone retching in the bushes. She looked at Tab. "Our first casualty of the night?"

"Sounds like it. Let me go check. I'll meet you back at the fire."

Ruth and Liz were pouring shots of Fireball when she returned to the group. Liz smiled when she walked up. "Where's Tab?"

"She's rescuing someone from retching in the bushes." Cam looked up and didn't see Bugsy anywhere. "Probably Bugsy. I don't see her around."

"Okay, so she's riding in the bed of the truck on the way home," Ruth groaned. "If she's already sick, it's going to be a long night for her, especially after the shot."

Several moments later, Tab emerged with Bugsy walking slowly beside her, looking a bit green around the gills. Cam took a look at her and felt sorry for Bugsy. She knew she was going to have a rough night. She shook her head then helped Ruth and Liz pass out the shot glasses.

The fire was slowly dying but still put off enough light that Cam could see the faces of her teammates as they all turned toward Ruth.

"As the only senior on this year's team, it's my responsibility to welcome each of you to the team and to remind you that the rest of the upperclassmen and I are here to help you with school, playing ball, and life in general. What happens within the team, stays with us, so if you ever need to discuss anything, we are here for you. Geaux Tigers." She raised her glass to the chorus, then they downed their shots.

Bugsy drank her shot and swayed on her feet. "Okay, hotshot, it's time to get you in the back of the truck," Liz said and led her to it.

"I'd hate to be inside her head in the morning," Parker whispered in Cam's ear.

"Me too," Cam said and turned to find Parker only inches from her. She smiled and took a step back to add some distance between them.

"I think I'll ride in the back with Bugsy to make sure she doesn't fall out on the way home."

"Thanks, Parker. That's very kind of you."

"That's what teammates do." She grinned and went to help Liz get Bugsy in the truck bed as others began leaving the circle.

Cam looked at Tab. "What do we use to put the fire out?"

"The ice water from the coolers will work. I don't think there's but a few beers left anyhow."

Ruth came up beside them. "I've already put the last six in a small cooler for you and slipped it behind your seat. If you'll help me carry the cooler, we can douse the fire, and I'll take this group home."

"It looks like everyone's ready to call it a night," Tab agreed.

"What can I do to help?"

"You can check around and make sure we didn't miss any trash, Cam. I think Liz and I've gotten most everything, but a second look won't hurt."

"I'm on it, boss."

Cam found two more bottles and placed them in the bag in Ruth's truck, then heard the hiss fill the air as the cool water hit the hot coals. Tab poured the contents of the second cooler after Ruth spread the embers.

Tab turned to Ruth. "I'll stay and make sure it's out." Cam walked up to them. "You can wait for me or ride back with Ruth."

Cam grinned. "I believe I'll wait if that's okay."

"Thanks." Tab smiled.

101

"See you in the morning for breakfast?" Ruth asked.

"Absolutely," Tab answered. "Be careful on the way back."

"Will do. Y'all be careful too."

†

When the rest of the team had left, Tab took a stick to stir the ashes. When she was satisfied the fire was out, she joined Cam on a log. "I think it's safe to go. It's still early. You up for a short ride?"

"That sounds good. It's turned out to be nice weather tonight."

Tab drove them a few miles farther south and turned onto another small path that led even closer to the water. She pointed the car north and they could see the lights of the Baton Rouge skyline.

"Beautiful," Cam whispered.

"Yes, it is." Tab relaxed back in her seat as they enjoyed the view. "You and Parker seemed to hit it off pretty good."

"She's pretty nice. Should I take her one of your applications?"

"She is very attractive and those green eyes are amazing, but I've decided to hold off on the applications for now."

"Oh really, why's that?"

"I'm hoping you'll come to realize we have chemistry between us." Cam chuckled and Tab cocked her head. "You think I'm wrong?"

"You're the second person tonight to mention that. Parker was the first. She said we couldn't keep our eyes off each other."

"She's right. Whenever you're near, my eyes are drawn to you."

"You realize you would have to teach me everything."

102

"I'm patient, and I'm betting you will be a great student." Tab smiled.

Cam leaned over until her face was inches from Tab's. "Kiss me, please."

Cam closed her eyes and an eternity seemed to pass before the softness of Tab's lips brushed hers. She let out a low moan when Tab's tongue slowly glided across her lips, searching for an invitation to deepen the kiss. Cam's instinct took over as her lips parted, and Tab's tongue swept into her mouth, the cinnamon from the Fireball shot still vibrant on it. Tab's hand was at the base of her neck, caressing her skin as their tongues danced sensually. Cam wanted more. She hungered for Tab's skin next to hers, and more of her delicious kisses. She was nearly breathless when they ended the first kiss. Her eyes fluttered open and she found Tab smiling at her.

"Wow. That was nice."

"Yes, it was." Tab leaned back in to kiss her again, and Cam's body responded. After several minutes of deep kissing, Tab sat back in her seat and reached over for Cam's hand. "As badly as I want you at this moment, I want us to be patient and be completely sober before we go any further. Is that okay with you?"

Cam couldn't wipe the grin off her face and nodded. "I think that's a good decision." She lifted Tab's hand to her lips and kissed across her knuckles. "Thank you. Let's go home."

✝

"I know we're going to take things slow, but I want to sleep next to you tonight. Is that okay?"

Tab grabbed Cam's hand and led her inside the apartment, then kicked the door closed behind them. She pulled her close and smiled. "Of course it is. I prefer sleeping naked. Is that okay?"

Heat rose to Cam's face. "That's what I was hoping to hear."

"Thank God. I hate sleeping in clothes, but I didn't want to scare you into fleeing back to the bayou."

Cam smirked. "That's not likely to happen."

They took turns in the bathroom, and when Cam emerged, she found Tab naked and lying on the bed. The sight of her lean body threatened to take her breath. "Damn, you're even more beautiful without clothes."

"See, I knew you'd be a quick learner. Come here, Ms. Smooth Talker."

"Should I blow out the candle?"

"Not just yet. I want to see all of you before we go to sleep."

Cam smiled as Tab turned on her side and propped up her head with her hand as she stretched out on the bed. Tab's eyes took in the length of her body and she appeared to enjoy every curve. "You are truly beautiful. No wonder you drive Bugsy wild," she teased.

"I've just never seen her as anything but a competitor. I can't even say we've grown to be close friends over the years we've known one another."

"I hope we will become that and much more," Tab said. "You can blow out the candle now, before I'm tempted to do more than just look."

Cam chuckled as she leaned up and with a soft puff brought darkness to the room.

"I noticed you're a side sleeper. Would you mind if I spooned you?"

Tab chuckled. "You've been secretly stalking me at night?"

"No, but when I wake up at night and hear your purring, I look and you're always facing one side or the other."

"Spoon away, then, John Boy," Tab said and rolled away from Cam. Cam held her breath, unsure if she could stand the feel of Tab's naked body pressed into hers. She let the breath out slowly as Tab's body molded perfectly into hers. She draped her arm across Tab's hip and felt the soft warmth of her skin. *Please let sleep come quickly tonight.*

Cam waited for Tab to roll onto her side, then carefully snuggled in behind her. Sleeping next to Tab was a new and exciting experience, and Cam felt comforted by how well their bodies molded together. *It's like we're two puzzle pieces that have finally found their mate.* She draped an arm across Tab's body, and her fingertips brushed across her smooth, warm skin, sending a shiver through Cam. She was positive Tab felt it.

"Are you okay?"

"Yes, I'm just enjoying the new sensations of being next to you probably a bit too much." She rested her head next to Tab's and knew her warm breath kissed Tab's neck as she spoke. "Good night, Mary Ellen."

Tab's tense body slowly relaxed as she drifted off to sleep. Cam concentrated on matching Tab's breathing, which helped her relax and follow her into sleep.

CHAPTER EIGHT

They shifted positions sometime during the night, and when Cam woke to find their bodies entwined, she carefully extracted herself from Tab's embrace and climbed from the bed. Her kidneys were screaming for relief and she wanted to go for a run to process all these new feelings. Running always helped clear her head.

Tab moaned when she left the bed. "Is it morning already?"

"It's barely six, but I need to go for a run. Go back to sleep, and when I get back, we can meet the others for breakfast."

"Do you want some company?"

"I'd normally say yes, but you look way too comfortable right now. Get some more sleep and I'll wake you when I get back." Cam leaned down and kissed her softly on the lips.

"Have a good run, then, and I'll see you when you return. Thanks for the kiss."

"My pleasure," Cam answered on her way to the bathroom. She emptied her bladder, then dressed in running clothes and shoes, brushed her teeth, then grabbed her ball cap and slipped quietly out the door. The hallway was quiet as she walked toward the front exit. She passed Ruth coming inside.

"Good morning," Cam said as she held the door open for her. "Out making a coffee run, I see."

"Yes'm, my Sunday morning ritual to hit Starbucks so Liz can wake up with a great cup of coffee. What are you doing up so early?"

"I'm going for a run to help process some thoughts."

"All good thoughts, I hope. Do they have anything to do with that sexy roommate of yours?"

Heat rose up her neck. Damn she hated blushing. "Maybe." She grinned.

"I hope you get things all worked out. Tab's a great person and I know she thinks highly of you."

"Only time will tell. Better get a move on before your coffee turns cold." Cam watched Ruth disappear and closed the door before she started walking to warm up her legs.

The sun wasn't fully up yet and the morning was relatively cool for this time of year. The birds were awake and singing, apparently enjoying the cool morning too. Cam stretched out her legs and started out at a slow jog, her feet leading her toward the softball diamond. Her mind was absorbed with thoughts of Tab and their potential relationship. Just the thought of a relationship was exciting and terrifying at the same time. She'd never dated much in high school, so the possibility of having a lover was mind-boggling. She was moving along at a quick pace and didn't notice the car that was driving beside her until she heard the whine of an electric motor. When she turned to it, the window rolled down and her coach smiled out at her.

"You're up mighty early this morning," she called out.

Cam slowed to a stop and looked at her. "I needed a run this morning."

"Everything okay? I figured you'd all be sleeping in this morning after a night at the river."

"Yes, ma'am, everything's good. We had a great time last night and everyone made it home safely. Where are you off to so early?"

"I wanted to get a head start on this week's practice schedule. You look like you've stayed in excellent shape over the summer."

"A lot of hard work keeps you in good shape. I've been trying to run a few days a week too. Is it true we don't start hitting and fielding until after Thanksgiving?"

Coach smiled. "Anxious to start wailing on some balls?"

"Yes, ma'am, I usually hit year-round when I can."

"The first couple of months we usually focus on fitness, but I'll make you a deal. If the team's in top shape by Halloween, we'll start hitting and fielding practice three days a week. I want you all to be hungry to hit the ball, but I can see you already have that drive."

"Thanks, Coach. I'll do what I can to challenge and motivate the others. May I share our deal with them?"

"If it'll help to motivate them, yes, go for it. Enjoy your run, Cam. See you Wednesday."

"Thanks, Coach. Have a good day."

When Cam realized her run had taken her to the softball field, she walked to the infield. She was excited to begin practice, and even more excited to start the season. She took a slow jog around the bases, then closed the gate behind her and started for home.

†

108

Tab walked out of the bathroom with a towel around her waist as Cam entered the apartment.

"Damn, I've got good timing," Cam said.

"Welcome back. I thought I'd go ahead and shower so we can go feed that beast of yours as soon as you're ready. Did you have a good run?"

"I did, and I ran into Coach. She said if we can have the team in top physical shape by Halloween, we can start batting and fielding practice three days a week."

"Damn, Coach has never agreed to that before. How'd you do it?"

"I just told her I was eager to start hitting, so we gotta get everybody in good shape."

"That sounds great to me. Go hit the shower, and we'll eat."

"First things first," Cam said, then pulled Tab close for a kiss. "I've been thinking about that for the last two miles."

"I'm going to get you up every morning for a run if that means I can get such a nice kiss. But go now, you're sweaty," she teased.

Cam laughed and pulled the towel from around Tab's waist as she took off for the bathroom. "Mmh, such a damn nice ass you have, Mary Ellen."

"Eat your heart out, John Boy," she called after her.

Cam could hear Tab laughing until she closed the door. She stripped out of her running clothes to enjoy a long, hot shower.

✝

They spent the rest of the day on the couch watching movies, frequently interrupted by slow, passionate kisses. Cam was a quick study, and by the time they finished dinner, Tab was so turned on she was quivering uncontrollably. She had two options to resolve her dilemma. One, she could send Cam out on an errand and take care of her raging hormones herself, or she could get Cam in bed and ravish her body. Tab was afraid she couldn't restrain herself in her current condition. Never before had she wanted someone so bad she physically hurt, but Cam had her walking that razor's fine edge. She decided on option one.

As they walked back from the cafeteria, Tab pulled Liz back to chat for a minute. "Liz, I'm in a bad way and I need your help."

"You're pregnant?" Liz teased.

"No, dammit, but that might be easier. If I were a guy, I'd have a horrible case of blue balls. Cam has me so turned on, I'm shaking on the inside and I don't trust myself. Will you please ask her to go to the store to pick up some ice cream for us? I need a few minutes of private time, to see if I can settle down."

Liz let out a laugh, then slapped a hand over her mouth, but not before Ruth and Cam glanced back at her with questioning looks. "I'm sorry, Tab. I know it isn't funny, but you have to admit, it kinda-sorta is."

"I'll laugh with you later, but right now I need a release. Please, Liz."

"Okay, okay." She smirked. "Mint chocolate chip for you?"

"Anything, just take your time getting back here."

"You got it, my friend. Hey, Cam," she called as she rushed to catch up with her and Ruth, who had walked ahead.

They stopped and Cam turned to Liz. "What's up?"

"Will you go to the store with me? Hot Stuff back there thinks we need some ice cream tonight."

"Uh, sure, no problem. Do you know what kind she likes?"

"Her favorite is mint chocolate chip if they have it. What can I get you, my love?" she asked Ruth.

"Rocky road or butter pecan. Either will work for me. You want to take the truck?" She pulled out her keys.

"That would be great. See y'all in a bit. C'mon, Cam." Liz led her to the truck as Tab and Ruth walked toward the apartment.

"What the hell is going on?" Ruth asked Tab.

"I'll tell you later." Tab rushed into the apartment, leaving a confused Ruth standing in the hall.

†

As they drove away, Cam asked Liz, "Is Tab okay? She looked a bit distressed."

"Yes, she's going to be fine. I think all the rich food we've been eating lately has gotten to her digestive system and she didn't want you to smell the aftereffects. *What the fuck? I couldn't have come up with anything better than that for an excuse? Just hope it works.*

"So you're telling me she didn't want me around for a major poop session?"

"Uh, yes, that's basically it. She didn't want to be embarrassed or embarrass you."

"No wonder you were having a hard time trying not to laugh. That woman is so silly," Cam said. "Are we really getting ice cream?"

"Why hell yes, we can't miss out on an opportunity for ice cream."

Cam just shook her head. "What will you gals think up next?"

"Only the good Lord knows," she answered. "Have you seen Bugsy today?"

111

"Just after lunchtime. She was still a bit nauseous and white as a sheet. Said she was up until three worshipping the porcelain goddess."

"Ouch, poor Bugsy."

"A hard lesson learned. I believe she'll drink a bit less next time, if there is a next time."

"Trust me, there will be a next time. We're college students, remember. It's our right to party." She turned into the lot at a local grocery chain. "Did I hear you telling Ruth you were going home next weekend to bring your baby sister to the ball game?"

"Yeah, Tab said she'd give up her ticket so Sandy can go."

"There's no need for that. She can use mine and I'll wait for y'all back at home. I don't care that much for football, but Ruth loves it, so I go for her. But if Sandy is football crazy like she sounds, Ruth won't miss me a bit."

"Thanks, Liz. I'd really hate for Tab to miss the game."

"No problem, my friend. Now let's go find some ice cream."

†

It had been some time since Tab had masturbated, but just like riding a bike, she soon remembered what her body responded to best. She wasn't shocked to find that she was soaking wet and ready to be touched when she shed her shorts and spread out on the bed. She closed her eyes and imagined Cam's fingers were deep inside her as she pressed her thumb firmly against her aching clitoris. Her trembling grew even more uncontrollable as she stroked her G-spot with her fingertips and the intense orgasm she had fought to control burst from her.

"Oh fuck yes," she cried as she broke out in a sweat. She removed her fingers and lay there for several minutes trying to catch her breath, her heart pounding as the quivering became a sensation of comforting bliss. "Holy shit, that was intense. There's no sleeping on these sheets tonight," she said, then broke into a laugh. "Damn, she's got me all tore up."

She looked at the clock and knew the others would be back from the store soon, so she stripped the sheets and tossed them in the hamper, followed by the rest of her clothing. She needed a shower to rinse off the smell of the orgasm and possibly relax further. Tab turned on the water and grabbed fresh clothes. Hopefully she could shower and get there before they returned.

✝

"Let's go, Romeo," Liz hollered as they walked past the apartment door.

"I'll be right down," Tab answered.

Liz opened the door to her apartment, and Ruth was sitting on the couch watching the Saints game. She gave Liz a curious look, but her lover smiled and shook her head, so Ruth didn't ask what was going on.

That's my smart woman. Liz smiled and shot a wink to Ruth. "We couldn't decide for you, so I bought you both flavors."

"You know it won't go to waste. Is Tab on her way down?" The knock on the door answered her question. "Come on in," Ruth hollered.

"Thanks," Tab said as she slipped inside the door. "Man, am I starving."

"Did everything come out all right?" Cam asked.

113

Liz watched as Tab nearly turned purple with embarrassment. Tab had no idea that Liz hadn't told Ruth what was going on. A glance at Liz, who was shaking her head, didn't seem to ease her mind any. "Um, yeah, everything is fine now. Thanks. Did they have mint chocolate chip?"

"Yes, they did. Come on in and you can help me get the ice cream ready. Do you two have sodas in your fridge?"

"Yes, we do. Would you like some?" Cam offered, heading toward the door much to Tab's apparent relief.

"That would be great. Ice cream always makes me thirsty and I didn't think to pick any up." Liz glanced at Ruth, who had opened her mouth, probably to say they had a refrigerator full, when she got "the look" from Liz that warned her to not make a comment.

"I'll be right back," Cam said and left the apartment.

"Will someone please tell me what the hell is going on?"

"Later," Tab and Liz said.

"You didn't tell her, did you?"

"For goodness sake, no. I told her you were having tummy troubles and had to shit, and you didn't want her around to smell the aftereffects."

"Oh dear Lord, you couldn't think up anything better?"

"I didn't exactly have time to plan, my friend. Are you feeling better?"

"You wouldn't believe how much better. Thank you."

"Forget the damned bowl," Ruth growled and grabbed her pint of ice cream and a spoon before storming back to watch the game.

Liz and Tab shook with laughter. "What a crazy turn of events. So she got you all wound up?"

"You wouldn't believe just how bad. You're a lifesaver, my friend. I owe you big-time for this, and I hope Ruth won't be mad for long."

"No problem. As soon as y'all leave, I'll tell her everything and she'll probably wet herself laughing."

Cam returned carrying a six-pack of Coke.

Liz could barely stop grinning. "Grab two for you and Tab and I'll stick the rest in the fridge. Ruth has decided we're going primitive today, so grab your pint and a spoon. No bowls allowed."

"Works for me," Cam said and carried the drinks and her ice cream to the living room.

†

When the game ended, Cam and Tab returned to their apartment. Liz was in the kitchen rinsing off their spoons when Ruth came up behind her and hugged her. "I'm assuming you're going to tell me what the heck was going on earlier," she whispered, then kissed her neck.

Liz turned to face her lover and kissed her softly. "Seems like our good friend Tab had a good case of the 'blue balls,' as she put it. Cam had her so turned on, she was in a bad way and needed a release."

"Well that's got to be a first."

"She practically begged me to convince Cam to go to the grocery store to get ice cream, so she could um, take care of business and get some relief."

Ruth chuckled. "And you came up with the tummy-trouble story on the fly?"

"That's the only thing that popped into my head. You have to admit, though, that the look on Tab's face was priceless when Cam asked her if everything came out okay."

"It was definitely a Kodak moment," Ruth agreed. "So I take it they've been doing some experimenting?"

"Kissing and some light petting, but it had Tab tore up from the floor up."

"That is just too funny. You ready to go do some experimenting of our own?" She took Liz's hand and led her into their bedroom.

†

Cam immediately noticed Tab's stripped bed. "What happened here?"

"I spilled something on my sheets, so I'll have to remake my bed or we'll have to use yours tonight."

"We can use mine. I have three classes tomorrow, starting at eight. What about you?"

"I only have two, one at eight and another at ten."

"Can we meet for lunch after class? I've got a class at one, and then could we work out tonight?"

"I do believe that could be arranged."

"I'm used to playing every sport in high school, so not having something to practice every day is making me feel lazy."

Tab slipped her arms around Cam's waist. "I totally understand. I was a multiple-sport athlete too. Are you going to run in the morning?"

"No, I want to make sure I get a good breakfast before classes start."

"Don't be surprised if the first class or two releases early. The profs will share the class schedule and talk about the material they will cover over the semester. Are you nervous?"

Cam nodded. "A little bit. It's just the fear of the unknown. I think once I learn what will be expected of me, the more I'll relax."

"You're going to do just fine."

Cam reached for Tab's hand. "Thanks for a great weekend."

"It was fun. The first of many I hope to share with you."

"I hope so too."

"Will you snuggle with me tonight?"

"I was hoping you'd ask. You ready to hit the sack?"

"Yeah, we have a busy week ahead of us. I'm really excited to meet your family. I hope they'll like me."

Cam led her to the bed. "No worries there, they're gonna love you. I have to warn you that Sandy may be crushing on you after next weekend."

"Oh really?"

"I think she's a lesbian in the making."

"Aww, I'll do my best to charm her socks off, then."

"That won't be hard at all for you to do."

"Can I assume that I have you charmed, then?" She smirked.

Cam pulled her down to the bed with her. "In the very best of ways," she answered as she wrapped her arms around Tab.

CHAPTER NINE

The week passed quickly. Cam was relieved to finally start the workouts, and when Friday came, she and Tab drove home to meet the family and pick up Sandy for the ballgame on Saturday. When they arrived in town, Cam gave her the five-minute tour before giving Tab directions to her home. It was an early-release day for Sandy, and when Tab turned into the drive, they found her walking the short distance home.

Sandy turned as the sleek, black car approached, and squealed when she saw Cam in the passenger seat. Tab slowed to a stop beside her.

"What a beautiful car," she told Tab.

"Thanks. You must be Sandy. I'm Cam's roommate, Tab."

"Hiya, Tab," Sandy replied in a bashful tone.

"How's it going, Squirt?" Cam asked.

"Better now that you're home. I've got my bag packed. When are we leaving?"

"Do you think I can visit with the rest of the family for a bit and introduce them to Tab?"

Sandy grinned the same lopsided grin as Cam had. "I reckon, if we have to. I'm just so excited about spending the weekend with y'all."

"It'll be fun, I promise," Cam assured her. "Hop in."

Cam opened the door and Sandy climbed in the backseat. "This is one sweet ride."

Cam smiled at Tab. "Onward, please, ma'am."

✝

Tab drove past a cane field and saw a man cutting. He looked up and smiled at them and lifted his hand in a wave. He was handsome, and she understood where Cam and Sandy got their looks. She followed Cam's direction, and pulled up behind a battered truck and killed the engine. A woman was sitting on the front porch shucking corn and looked up at their approach. She set the bowl of corn to the side and stood, wiped her hands on her apron, then started toward the car.

"Welcome home, baby," she said when Cam stepped out of the car, and hugged her close. When she released Cam, she smiled at Tab. "You must be Tab. Welcome, we've heard so much about you."

"It's nice to meet you, Mrs. St. Angelo."

"Please, call me Camille, or Mama like everyone else."

"Yes, ma'am," she answered and accepted Camille's hug.

"Are y'all hungry or thirsty?"

"I think Dad could use an RC. He looks hot out there. Squirt, will you run inside and get some, and we'll go check on him?"

"Sure, Cam," Sandy answered and disappeared into the house.

119

"Do you want to stay up here with Mama or walk out to the cane field? You might get dirty," she teased.

"Believe it or not, I have been in a cane field before," Tab huffed.

"You're from Monroe, is that right, Tab?"

"Yes, ma'am. There's a cane field or two along the way."

"Here I thought you were just a city girl," Cam joked.

"I got your city girl," Tab said and punched Cam in the shoulder.

"Ouch, you big brute, that hurt."

"Are you getting sissified, Cam?" Sandy asked as she stepped back through the door.

"No way, man," Cam answered. "But she does punch harder than you."

"See if you can get your dad to take a break. He's been cutting cane all day, waiting for T and Wanda to get home from school to help him load."

"Yes, ma'am, I'll see what I can do."

"Come on, Squirt, let's take City Girl to da fields."

"Okay, but here, you take your drinks first. My arms are freezing."

"Now who's getting sissified?"

"Not me," Sandy answered.

Camille eased her body back down in the chair to finish the corn. Sandy grabbed Tab's hand and led her off the porch. "C'mon, it's this way."

†

Ronny stopped cutting when he heard the laughter of the three young women heading toward him. He looked up to see his two daughters and Cam's roommate. Cam looked overjoyed as she chatted with the others. She seemed to have a glow around her.

"Hey there, ladies," he called out.

Sandy ran ahead and handed him a cold drink. "Thanks, I sure needed that," he said when he took the bottle. He wiped his sweaty hand on his pants and held it out to the young woman beside Cam. "You must be Tab."

Tab took his hand firmly and gave it a nice shake. "Yes, sir, I am. Nice to meet you."

"Welcome to our bayou." He looked at Cam. "You're looking good, baby girl. Is school going okay for you?"

"I survived my first week, so that's a start. How much more cane you planning to cut?"

"I'm just about tuckered out for the day. Your sisters will be home soon and can help me load the trailer."

"I can help you, Dad."

"No, you have to drive back to Baton Rouge to get ready for the big game. Your sisters and I can handle this."

"I know, but I worry about you out here in this heat."

"I'm thinking I'm going to drive the tractor and let the three of them load."

Cam nodded. "That's a great idea. Can you come sit on the porch and visit a bit before they get home?"

"That I can do," he agreed and followed them across the field. "Are you making sure Cam behaves herself?"

Tab gave him a warm smile. "She's been no problem at all. You raised a good one in her."

Ronny smiled back. "Yes, she's all a dad could ask for." He looked down at Sandy and ruffled her hair. "This little one is growing up to be just like her."

A look passed between the two women. "You're a very lucky dad, then," Tab told him.

"I think we're the lucky ones," Cam interjected. "Mama and you have sacrificed so much to raise us."

"That's not a sacrifice at all. It's just called being a family."

Cam draped an arm around his shoulders as they walked. "Careful, you're gonna get dirty and sweaty."

"I wash up well, Dad."

"That you do. You look good, and happy."

"Things couldn't be better," she answered, and he noticed that look pass between the two women again.

He smiled at Cam and wondered if she'd finally fallen in love. From the look on her face, he'd guess it was true. It didn't matter one bit to him if she loved a woman, as long as she was happy and treated right.

†

They all sat on the porch visiting until the other three girls got home from school. Ronny allowed them to chat with Cam and Tab for a few minutes before telling them to get dressed for work.

"Will you be able to stay for a crawfish boil on Sunday when you bring Sandy home? I can have it ready for a late lunch, if y'all can make it by then."

Cam looked at Tab. "From what I've heard of your boils, I'd be a fool to pass on that offer," Tab said.

"We'll make it happen, then," he answered and his face lit up with a smile.

Sandy paced nervously on the porch until Cam sighed. "Okay, Squirt, get your bag."

Camille smiled at her eldest. "She's very excited about this weekend. She hasn't stopped talking about it since your call last Sunday. She went directly to her room and packed her bag that night."

"I'm looking forward to it too. That stadium on game day is like nothing I've ever seen."

Ronny placed a hand on her shoulder. "It's a big one for sure and it looks like we've got a good team this year. That old Mad Hatter, he sure knows how to coach some football."

"Last week's game was more like a practice. I thought they would break one hundred even after he emptied the bench," Tab added. "This week should be a bit more competition."

Sandy rushed out of the house, a small bag in tow. "You got your bag. Did you get your money?"

"Yes, Dad, I did."

"Come give us a hug and have fun. Mind your sister," he warned.

"Yes, sir, I will." She hugged her parents. "Love ya, Mama and Dad."

"Love you too. Have fun and we'll see y'all on Sunday," Camille told her baby. "We'll be looking for you on TV."

"All right," she answered. "Can we go?"

Cam hugged and kissed her parents. "I reckon we have our marching orders. See you Sunday."

"It was nice meeting both of you," Tab said.

"Don't think you're getting off that easy, young woman," Camille said and pulled her into a hug. "I won't make you hug the dirty, old man, though."

"I wash up well too," she answered and hugged Ronny.

"Be careful," Ronny warned. "You'll have some of them crazy Texas drivers coming in for the game."

Tab chuckled. "Yes, sir, I will. I've got precious cargo on board."

"That ya do." He grinned.

Sandy raced ahead, placed her bag in the backseat, and climbed in behind Cam. She waved back to her parents and sisters as they pulled slowly out of the drive, and started driving to Baton Rouge. The wind whipped through their

123

hair as Tab drove, and Cam turned around. "You're not cold, are you?"

"No, this feels really good, like when we went on our trip," she answered.

"Okay, let me know if it gets to be too much. I don't want you sick before the game."

"Got it, Cam," she said as she brushed the hair out of her face.

Cam had dropped her ball cap on the floorboard, and she reached down to pick it up, then handed it to Sandy. "Here, this will help."

Sandy took the cap and put it on backward, the way she had seen Cam do so many times. Tab saw the grin on Cam's face and glanced in the mirror to see Sandy put it on backward, reminding her of the way Cam wears her cap. She looked over at Cam to see her grinning. *Yep, she's just like her sister. Adorable too.*

✝

They wove their way back onto campus between RVs and other massive vehicles coming for the early celebration. As they pulled into the lot, Liz and Ruth were just getting out of the truck.

"Welcome back. We thought we'd make some spaghetti tonight to welcome Sandy to the team," Liz said as Tab pulled up beside them. She looked into the backseat. "You have to be Sandy, you look just like Cam."

"Yes, ma'am," Sandy answered with a blush.

"You don't have to 'ma'am' me. I'm Liz, and this is Ruth. Is spaghetti okay with you?"

"It's one of my favorites."

"You want to come help me cook, then?"

Sandy looked at Cam. "Can I, Cam?"

Cam shrugged. "Fine with me. Sandy's an awful good cook. Can we help too?"

"You two can make us a nice salad, and Ruth will get garlic bread ready to go in the oven. I heard you like RC Cola. Is that true?"

"Yes, ma'am, it is," Sandy answered. "I mean Liz," she corrected.

"Why don't you take your bag to Cam's room, and when y'all get ready, come on over."

Cam placed her hand on Sandy's shoulder, "Sounds great, Liz. Give us about ten minutes to get her settled and have potty breaks, then we'll be over."

"You need help with those groceries?" Tab asked.

"Naw, we got this," Ruth chuckled.

Cam opened the door for the group and followed them inside.

"Wow, this place is huge," Sandy cried out when she entered the apartment.

"Toss your bag on my bed"—Cam pointed to her bed— "and the bathroom is right there," she said, pointing out another door. "You get to crash with me tonight, but no kicking."

"I'll try my best, Cam."

Tab waited until Sandy closed the door. "I'm going to miss snuggling with you."

"Me too, but I think we'll survive two nights."

"You might, but I'm going to be terribly jealous of Sandy. Would you mind if I give her something?"

Cam cocked her head. "You got her something?"

"Yeah, I overheard one of your conversations with her, so I thought I'd surprise you both."

"That's very sweet of you. Thank you."

When Sandy returned, Cam grinned. "Have a seat on the bed. I think Tab has a surprise for you."

Tab pulled out two wrapped boxes. "Actually, I have a surprise for both of you." She grinned as she handed them over.

Cam smiled at her. "You really didn't have to buy me anything."

"Just hush, and open the boxes."

Sandy didn't need another invitation. She carefully unwrapped the box and opened it to find a purple-and-gold softball jersey. The number fifteen was displayed on the back with *St. Angelo* written beneath it.

"This is mine?" Sandy squealed.

"Well, I only see one other St. Angelo in the room, and if she'll open her box, she'll find she has one too."

Cam ripped into the paper and opened the box to pull out an identical jersey in an adult size. "How on earth did you get these? They're wonderful."

"I have my connections." Tab grinned.

Sandy flew off the bed and hugged Tab. "Thank you so much. I'll wear it to the game tomorrow."

"Not tonight?" Cam asked.

"No, I don't want to run the risk of getting spaghetti on it."

"That makes perfect sense to me," Tab replied. "C'mon, let's hang it up."

Cam smiled as she watched Tab help Sandy hang the jersey in their closet, and then Sandy rushed back to get her sister's jersey.

Sandy grinned. "There, we're all set."

"Thanks, Tab." Cam hugged her close and kissed her softly on the lips.

Sandy squirmed with excitement. "Yes, thanks, Tab. I love my jersey. I can't wait to wear it to the game tomorrow." She hugged Tab and kissed her on the cheek.

126

"Okay, ladies, you are both quite welcome. Are we ready to go cook?"

"I'm so excited," Sandy said as they walked to the door together.

Cam smiled at Tab and whispered, "Thanks."

"Seeing her face was well worth the effort. Yours too."

✝

The team adopted Sandy as their little sister that weekend. She sat between Tab and Cam during the game, proudly wearing her jersey, and enjoyed every second of the game and festivities. Liz had steaming-hot pizzas waiting when they returned, and once she got her stomach full, Sandy snuggled into Cam on the couch and drifted off to sleep.

Liz smiled and whispered, "I do believe she's had a great weekend."

"She'll be talking about it for weeks," Cam assured her. "Thanks for helping me make it special for her," she said to her friends.

Ruth chuckled. "It's been great having her here this weekend. I hope there will be many others."

"I hope so too," Cam said and brushed a stray strand of hair from her face. "I think I'll go put her to bed."

"I'll go with you," Tab said as she stood. "You want me to carry her?"

"If you want. Thanks again for everything this weekend," she told Ruth and Liz as they walked to the door.

"Do you want to wake her to undress?" Tab asked as they entered the apartment.

"I'll just slip her shorts off. She can sleep in her jersey. I still can't believe you got those for us."

Tab stretched her out on the bed and watched as Cam slipped the shorts down her legs. "She's out like a light."

"She's had a busy weekend." Cam pulled the cover over Sandy, and nodded toward the bathroom.

Tab followed her, and as soon as the door closed behind them, Cam pulled her in for a kiss. "Damn, I needed that." She grinned when they broke the kiss.

"I needed that too. I hate to see her go, but I'll be glad to share a bed with you again."

"Me too. Let's crash and get up and then start for home after breakfast. I hope you're ready for a feast tomorrow, St. Angelo style."

"I'm looking forward to it," Tab answered and leaned in for another kiss. "Good night."

✝

Sandy hugged everyone goodbye before they left for home. The clouds hung low, and Cam was sure they wouldn't make it back before the rain arrived. As soon as Tab pulled the car to a stop, Sandy bounded out and ran in search of her dad to tell him all about her weekend. Cam could smell food cooking and knew the family would be in the backyard.

Camille looked up from her location in the kitchen and said, "Welcome home," when Tab and Cam entered the house carrying Sandy's bag. "Did you have a good weekend?"

"It was incredible and I think you'll be hearing about it for a few weeks," Cam answered as she bent down to kiss her mama's cheek. "What can I do to help?"

"I'm almost done here, so take Tab out and show her around the place and relax for a bit. The boil will be ready soon."

128

†

Once everyone was stuffed, Cam and Ronny wrapped up humongous plates for Ruth and Liz at Sandy's suggestion, and Cam smiled at her baby sister.

"I think you adopted a few more sisters this weekend," she said as she hugged her close.

"I had so much fun," Sandy purred. "I can't wait to visit again."

"We'll take a look at the schedule and see what we can set up," Cam promised.

Ronny turned his head at the sound of thunder rumbling across the bayou. "I'm not rushing you two off, but it's going to be pouring here soon. If you leave now, you might get ahead of the storm."

"Thanks for such a great meal," Tab said as she hugged Camille and Ronny.

"You're welcome here any time," Ronny said.

He and Sandy walked them out. Cam loaded the plates in the back of the car and turned to find Sandy frowning and on the verge of tears. She bent over and kissed her forehead. "Thanks for making it such a great weekend. We'll do it again soon, okay?"

Sandy hugged Cam and Tab. "Thanks again for my jersey."

"What jersey?"

"Tab bought matching jerseys for Cam and me," Sandy answered.

"Come on, you can show me. Drive safe, girls. Love y'all."

"Love y'all too," Cam answered and watched him lead Sandy back toward the house before his baby girl started crying. "We better go."

†

The rain caught them an hour from campus, and they got soaked running from the car, carrying the plates of food for Ruth and Liz.

"Let's drop these off and go get out of these wet clothes," Cam suggested.

They rushed down to Ruth and Liz's apartment and knocked. When Liz opened the door, she looked at them and grinned. "You two look like drowned rats."

"I know, but we wanted to drop these off as a thank-you from Sandy," Cam said as she offered Liz a plate.

"Oh my goodness, do I smell crawfish?" Ruth asked when she walked to the door.

Tab handed her a plate. "A thank-you from Sandy. She had a great weekend."

"Aw, your sister is so sweet. Damn you're wet." Ruth grinned.

"It's pouring outside, so we're going to get out of these wet clothes. Enjoy, ladies," Tab said and took Cam's hand.

Back inside their apartment, they removed their wet clothes and dried their skin as a chill set in to their bodies.

"Let's snuggle under the covers to get warm," Cam suggested.

"You won't get an argument from me," Tab said as she tossed the covers open on her bed. She climbed in and pulled Cam into her, wrapping her arms around her. "Damn, this feels good."

Before she could speak again, Cam covered her mouth with a deep kiss as she rolled on top of Tab. Their bodies heated quickly as they lay skin to skin, and Tab couldn't prevent the moan from escaping. Her desire was escalating at a phenomenal rate, and she was quivering uncontrollably. Her inability to control her emotions scared her.

"This probably isn't a good position for us to be in right now," she warned. "I might not be able to stop."

"I don't want you to stop tonight."

"What did you say?"

"I said, I don't want you to stop tonight, Tab. I want to make love with you."

Tab rolled Cam onto her back and kissed her sweetly. "Are you sure?"

Cam smiled up at her, took Tab's hand, and placed it between her legs. "My body and heart are ready for you."

Tab thought she would pass out from the sheer excitement as her hand covered Cam's heated, wet mound. She trembled with need and her hand shook as she lifted it to her lips to taste the glistening moisture coating her fingers. "Damn, I want you so much."

"Take me," Cam whispered, her voice filled with emotion.

Tab had longed to hear those words. She teased and caressed Cam's body with mouth and hands as she explored inch after inch of the woman she was growing to love. Her teeth nibbled a nipple, pebbled with arousal, and Cam groaned.

"I want to make it feel so good for you," Tab said, her heated breath flowing over Cam's breast as she stroked her hand down the front of Cam's body. She gently parted Cam's desire soaked-lips as she ran her fingertips through the wetness soaking the layers of her opening, teasing Cam's body as Cam opened her legs wider, inviting Tab to enter. She slipped a fingertip inside the silky folds and Cam gasped.

"You okay?"

"Hell yes, that feels so good."

Tab ran her tongue across Cam's lips. "It will feel even better in just a few minutes." Tab entered her more deeply with a second finger, and Cam's muscles twitched from her presence. Her tongue danced with Cam's as she sank her fingers into the welcoming wetness. It was her turn to moan, deeply inside Cam's mouth, as strong muscles clenched her fingers. Her arousal soared and Cam's hips lifted off the bed, urging her deeper. Tab withdrew her fingers and sunk them deep inside Cam, picking up a slow rhythm. Cam rolled her hips as she filled their mouths with vibration, her moans growing louder. Tab's thumb grazed over Cam's swollen clit, and Cam shuddered. She broke the kiss and locked eyes with Cam. "Come for me, baby."

Tab felt Cam explode with turbulent pleasure, and she stilled her fingers, allowing Cam to enjoy the sensation. Tab's every small movement caused another wave of tremors, so she rested her fingers as she kissed Cam deeply.

"That was so beautiful," Tab whispered when Cam calmed. She carefully extracted her fingers from the silky wetness. "You ready for more?"

She smiled when Cam nodded, then kissed her way down Cam's front.

†

Tab's tongue left a burning trail of desire in its wake. Cam had never dreamed she could react the way she just had, but when Tab's tongue entered her for the first time, sliding deep into her core, she felt like her mind would explode with pleasure. Tab teased her to peak after peak, slowly easing off until Cam grabbed the sheets and felt her hips rise. Tab's hands slid under her ass as Tab buried her face and feasted in her wetness. Cam's body exploded again, releasing a flood of wetness onto Tab's face that she greedily lapped, extending

Cam's orgasm for several long seconds. When Cam fell exhausted back to the bed, Tab moved to lie atop her, kissing her deeply, sharing the taste of her pleasure.

Cam thought she would come again when Tab pressed their bodies together. When she tasted her wetness in Tab's mouth, her body responded, trembling uncontrollably. She wanted and needed more.

Tab ground into her, their bodies moving in unison. Cam grabbed her ass, thrusting up to meet her, and released a shuddering orgasm on top of her. Tab moved to the side, straddled Cam's leg, and placed Cam's right hand between her legs. Cam entered her with two fingers, and Tab thrust onto them as she also penetrated Cam with deep strokes and their mouths melded in a fevered kiss. Tab exploded and thrust deeper as Cam joined her in release, then collapsed on the bed beside her lover, panting to catch her breath.

Excited by all the new sensations, Cam turned toward Tab. "I want to taste you."

Tab smiled and nodded.

Cam was a quick learner and explored Tab's body with her tongue, noting areas of sensitivity and she easily brought Tab to orgasm. Cam's moans of pleasure as she feasted on Tab's wetness added to the sensation of her probing tongue and fingers. Soon, Tab chuckled and pulled Cam up next to her.

"We won't be able to get out of bed tomorrow if we keep this up."

Cam snuggled into her. "I don't care if I have to crawl to class. That was incredible."

"Yes, it was. Well worth waiting for."

"I'm sorry for making you wait."

Tab lifted her face to look into Cam's eyes. "Don't be sorry. It had to be the right time for your first time."

"I will never forget this night."

"Neither will I, but it's late, so we'd better get some sleep."

Cam entwined her legs with Tab's and slipped into an exhausted slumber.

CHAPTER TEN

Cam enjoyed college life, but she lived for the hours she spent practicing and improving her physical conditioning. Coach was pleased at her team's motivation to reach the challenge to be in peak physical conditioning by Halloween, and as promised, they began hitting and fielding earlier than they normally would. Cam felt so relaxed and in love. This calmness transferred into her batting, and the increase in her power left Coach smiling like the Cheshire Cat.

Coach grinned at Cam as she stepped out of the batting cage. "I don't know what's changed you, Cam, but your technique at the plate has dramatically improved. Don't let it go to your head just yet, but I can't wait to see you hitting in a live game."

"I'll do my best to not disappoint you, Coach."

"I totally believe that, and I hope it's contagious."

†

Sandy and the rest of the family came down for two more games during football season, and Cam was delighted when Tab asked her to meet her family over Christmas break. Life was good, almost too good to be true. In a few short weeks, the team would start full daily workouts and the season would begin. She would realize one of her dreams: to play college softball in the SEC.

Before break started and they would leave for their homes, they made love deep into the night.

"Damn, I'm going to miss falling asleep in your arms every night," Tab said as she rolled onto her back next to Cam. "You're still coming up after Christmas, right? Mom and Dad are going to some social event in New Orleans for New Year's, so we'll have the house all to ourselves."

"That sounds great. I'm nervous about meeting your folks, though."

"Just relax and be yourself. Mom and Dad can be a bit stuffy at first, but they will love you."

Cam rolled onto her side. "That was your best effort at getting me to relax?"

"I'm sure you can tolerate a few days with them, and then we'll have the run of the place. I can't wait to get you into the hot tub," Tab said, wiggling her eyebrows.

"Now that's an offer too good to resist."

†

Tab woke the next morning to find Cam still curled around her. *So beautiful, and all mine.* She carefully lifted a strand of loose hair from Cam's face and tucked it behind her ear. Cam's eyes fluttered open and she smiled at Tab. "Good morning, lover."

She felt Cam's body coil and stretch, like a cat first waking from a nap. "Good morning to you. I slept in, didn't I?"

"Yes, but I enjoyed the extra time cuddling next to you. You can get up before the crack of dawn to run when you get back home."

"I won't need to run. I'm sure there is plenty I can help Dad with to give me a workout."

"Will I be too much of a pain if I call you every day?"

"You'll have to call after supper so I'll be sure to be near the phone."

"I think I have the solution for that." Tab climbed from the bed and walked to her closet. She pulled down a box and carried it back to the bed, then opened it as Cam sat up. "I hope you don't mind, but I bought a cell phone for you. That way we can talk anytime we want."

Cam looked at her. "You think of everything. Thanks, this will be perfect, but I insist on paying the bill."

"No bill. I got it on our friends-and-family plan." Tab grinned. "I've already got my number programmed in for you." She demonstrated how to use the phone and how to charge it. "Merry Christmas early," she said and kissed her. "Trust me, it's as much a gift for me as you. Now I know I can reach you when I need to hear your voice."

Looking a loss for words, Cam pulled Tab into her arms and kissed her. "I miss you already."

"Hopefully the time will pass quickly until we're together again."

Cam kissed her again. "Not fast enough for me."

"I'll call you when I make it to Monroe." Tab picked up her bag. "I love you."

She smiled at Tab. "I love you too."

"The sooner we start, the sooner we'll be together." Tab took her hand and grabbed Cam's bag. They walked out together and hugged before climbing into their vehicles to head for home.

†

Cam followed the sleek black convertible before she had to turn onto her route. She smiled the entire drive to Morganza, and when she pulled up next to her house, Sandy ran out to meet her.

She squealed, "You're finally back."

"Hiya, Squirt." Cam leaned down to pick up her sister and twirled her around. "I'm so glad to be here."

"I've missed you so much." Sandy smiled when Cam placed her back on the ground. "Did you finish Tab's present?"

"Almost," Cam answered. "Will you help me finish it tonight?"

Sandy grinned. "You know I will."

"Good, let's go see what Mama's cooking up." She pulled her bag from the back of the Jeep.

Sandy slipped her hand inside Cam's and they entered the house.

†

Christmas at the St. Angelos' was as festive as ever. Cam and her sisters helped their mama create a feast, and Christmas morning brought many needed items and surprises for everyone. Cam and Tab talked several times a day, both eager to reunite in a few short days. With Sandy's help, Cam finished Tab's gift, and Cam was excited to see her lover's reaction.

†

When everyone had gone to bed the night after Christmas, Cam was surprised by a knock on her door. She opened it to find Wanda and invited her sister inside.

"Hey, kiddo, is everything okay?"

"Yeah, Cam, I just wanted to talk with you if you have a few minutes."

"Sure, we can talk anytime."

Wanda blushed. "This isn't something I can talk about with anyone but you, and I hope you'll understand."

Cam cocked her head at her sister as they sat on her bed. "This sounds pretty serious."

Wanda looked away from her. "I need to ask your advice on something."

Cam smiled. "You know I'll help you if I can."

"It's about a girl," Wanda said. "Are you and Tab, you know…lovers?"

Cam had had no idea this would be the topic of conversation, but she wasn't in the habit of lying to her family and she wouldn't start now. Besides, if Wanda was intuitive enough to ask, she probably knew the answer already. "Yes, we are, Wanda."

"Is she like your first girlfriend or were you in love with Bren?"

"Yes, Tab is my first. I had a crush on Bren, but it never went any further."

"How did you know you were a lesbian?"

Cam thought about her answer for several seconds. "I really didn't think about being a lesbian, to be honest. As you know, I didn't date much in high school and was more interested in sports than I was chasing after boys."

"Yeah, I kinda get that."

"So, when I met Tab, I was attracted to her as a person, not just because she was female. We have some things in

139

common, such as a love of sports, but we are from completely different worlds. I think we fell in love partly because of our differences. Does that make any sense?"

Wanda smiled. "I think I follow you. I see this girl, I feel like I've got a herd of elephants in my stomach."

"Do you know if she has feelings for you?"

"Yes, I'm pretty sure she does, but we haven't done any experimenting yet."

"Is she in your class?"

"No, she's a year ahead of me, but she's on the basketball team. She's also a shortstop, just like you."

"Do I know her?"

"No, she transferred into our school this year. Her parents divorced and her mom has family here, so they've moved in with her grandma."

"What has she done to give the impression she's attracted to you?"

"She touches me a lot. Damn, that didn't come out right."

Cam chuckled. "It's okay, but I think you need to explain it better."

"Whenever we're together, she seems to have a need to be close to me. On the bus on ball trips, she always sits so close that we're touching. Sometimes, when the bus gets dark, she holds my hand, or lays her head on my shoulder."

How sweet. Wanda is so much more in tune with her feelings than I was at her age. "Have you talked to her about how you feel?"

"Not yet. I was hoping you could give me some advice."

"Well, Tab's a year older than me and she'd had a girlfriend before we met, so she had some experience, which made it easier for me. You're fourteen and starting to blossom into a young woman, and I'm sure the surge of hormones has you confused about some of your feelings. Heck, mine still do," she admitted.

"I'm not a kid." Wanda frowned.

"That's not at all what I meant. Maybe I was a late bloomer, because you seem more advanced in understanding your feelings than I was at your age."

Wanda smiled and appeared to relax. "So, what do I do?"

"What does your heart tell you?"

"That I think I love her. Her touch, and the way she looks at me makes my heart race like crazy. I've never felt about anyone like that."

"That definitely sounds like you got the love bug," Cam agreed. "Dad won't let you spend a night out on the Island alone for a few more years, and a sleepover here definitely won't give you any privacy. Can you hold off until I come home this summer? Just take things slow until you really understand your feelings for one another?"

"That seems like forever."

"You have forever in front of you. There's no need to rush into anything you may not be completely prepared for, you know. Has Mama given you the birds and the bees talk yet?"

"Yes, Cam, I got that two years ago."

"Damn, have I gotten old?"

"No, but the rest of us are growing up too."

"Well you know how Mama always preaches about not having sex with boys until you're sure you're in love and ready for marriage?"

"Yes, we hear it often now that Karen is dating Buster's brother, Jeffrey."

"What? When did that happen?"

"Months ago, Cam." She chuckled. "You've been away at college, remember?"

"But you all can't grow up yet. You're still my baby sisters." Cam shook her head. "But, anyhow, back to my point. Another girl can't get you pregnant, but you need to understand the hurt that you can experience. You need to decide if your feelings for her are genuine, or just a crush like I had with Bren. The way I loved Bren is much different than the way I love Tab. Bren will always be my childhood friend, but it would have been a mistake to try to have more with her."

Cam sighed. "I guess what I'm try to say is don't rush things and see where fate takes you. There's no need to jump into a physical relationship. When I come home for summer break, we can invite her out for a sleepover at the hunt camp if you're still having feelings for her."

"Will Tab be there too?"

"I'm sure she'd love a sleepover."

"You seem really happy whenever Tab's around."

"She makes me very happy. She's patient with me and is teaching me how to love."

Wanda looked up at Cam with her eyes sparkling. "I hope Logan and I will have that."

Cam smiled. "Logan, huh?"

"Yeah, her name is Logan."

"I look forward to meeting her one day soon."

"Are you ready to go see Tab?"

Cam reached over and pulled Wanda into a hug. "I love being home with you all, but I'm ready to see her again. We've talked several times every day I've been home, but the sound of her voice makes me miss her even more."

"You've got it bad, huh?"

"Yeah, I reckon I do." Cam kissed the top of her head. "You know you can call and talk to me anytime, right?"

"Not if Sandy's anywhere around," Wanda chuckled.

"I'll be sure to ask specifically for you after I talk to Sandy, then, so maybe she'll let you talk."

She smiled. "I'd like that."

"Do you feel better?"

"Yes, just talking about her has helped. I'm still unsure of things, but like you said, I'll take it slow."

"Trust me, when it's the right time, you'll know."

"Thanks, Cam. Love ya."

"Love you too. Sweet dreams."

†

When the day arrived for Cam to leave for Monroe, Sandy watched Cam pack her bag, with teary eyes.

Cam sat down on the bed beside her. "You know softball season will start up very shortly after we return to school, and most of our games are on the weekends. We'll work something out to get you down for as many of our home series as we can."

"I'd like that," Sandy said and wiped at her eyes.

"You wanna carry my bag while I say goodbye to everyone?"

Cam hugged each of her family and promised to return home for a weekend prior to the season starting. "I'll be seeing you soon." She kissed Sandy on the head after lifting her bag into the Jeep. "Love ya, Squirt."

"Love you more."

"No way, man." She grinned.

Cam climbed behind the wheel and waved as she watched Sandy in the rearview mirror, waving until she turned onto the hard road heading north.

†

Cam slowed as she checked the address Tab had written down. The sprawling antebellum home with the large circular driveway was the right place. She smiled when she saw Tab's Mustang parked in the drive. *Damn, I'm way out*

143

of my league here. The mansion loomed ahead, filling her windshield with its massive size.

"Quite a spread for three people," she said as she pulled to a stop behind Tab's car.

The front door flew open and Tab rushed out to great her. "Damn, I'm glad you finally made it."

"I missed you too," she answered as she stepped out of the Jeep and hugged Tab.

When Tab kissed her, Cam couldn't hide the surprised look on her face.

"Relax, Mom and Dad are having lunch in town. C'mon, let's get you inside so I can have many more of those kisses before they return."

Cam grabbed her bag and took the hand Tab offered. She followed her into the pristine home and Tab pulled her up a large spiral staircase straight out of *Gone with the Wind*. "Do you ever get lost in this house?"

"It can be overwhelming at first."

"All of this for three people?"

"Welcome to the Fortner Mansion. You go big or you go home." Tab chuckled.

"This is beyond big. This place is huge."

Tab opened a door and pulled Cam inside. Cam was surprised to realize the large room was Tab's bedroom.

"This room is over half the size of our whole house." Before she could comment further, Tab covered her mouth in a deep kiss. Cam dropped her bag and pulled Tab into her arms.

When they broke the kiss, Cam was nearly breathless but did manage to say, "I guess you really did miss me."

"Never doubt that I did. I thought Christmas would never be over."

"We had a great holiday. I wish you could have been there with us."

"Maybe next year I will. I'm sure the holidays at your home are much more joyous than they are here."

"We had a blast. The food was fantastic and everyone was pleased with their gifts."

"I got a fancy new laptop to help with school, some new clothes, and jewelry. Mom and Dad are going on a three-week European cruise next spring."

"Why the frown?"

"They scheduled the cruise during the Women's College World Series, so if we make it they won't even attend."

"Not if, *when* we make it," Cam corrected. "My family can't afford to make the trip, but you can bet they'll be watching every game we play."

Tab brushed a strand of hair away from Cam's face. "I envy you for the loving family you have. I've never felt the love that surrounds your entire family, that they don't hesitate with someone they've barely met."

"I've been blessed. That's for sure."

"Do you want to see your Christmas gift?"

"I thought the cell phone was my gift."

"Hardly." Tab walked over to a cabinet, pulled out a long box, and handed it to her. "Merry Christmas." She watched as Cam carefully removed the wrapping paper and opened the box, then gasped as her eyes lit up. "Do you like it?"

"I love it," Cam said as she gently pulled out a gold rope necklace with a solid gold whale's fluke charm. Two diamonds graced the outer fins.

"It's supposed to bring luck to the wearer."

"It's gorgeous. It must have cost a fortune."

"You're worth every penny. Here, let me help you put it on." Tab took the necklace, slipped it around Cam's neck, and fastened the clasp.

Cam glanced in the mirror. "It really is beautiful." She kissed Tab. "My gift to you is nowhere near this elaborate."

145

"Anything from you will be special to me, even a lump of coal."

"It's not a lump of coal," she said as she pulled a wrapped box from her bag and handed it to Tab. She watched with an anxious expression as Tab removed the paper to reveal a shoebox. "I thought you needed new slippers."

The box was too heavy to be slippers as it rested in Tab's hands. She carefully removed the lid and gasped. "It's Mike the Tiger. Did you make this?"

"Yes, I carved him out of some cypress wood, and Sandy helped me polish and wrap him for you."

"This is the best gift I've ever gotten, Cam. No one has ever made anything for me before, and he's beautiful."

"I'm glad you like him."

"I love him."

Cam smiled as Tab glided her fingers over the smooth wood.

"He's so beautiful," Tab said as a tear ran down her cheek.

"Oh, baby, don't cry," Cam said as she pulled her close.

†

They were sitting on Tab's bed and Cam had her laughing at stories of the Christmas she had shared with her family when Tab's parents returned home. They walked through the open door, and Cam could feel Tab stiffen as the closing of the door announced their presence. Tab's eyes turned to focus on her bedroom door.

"Mom and Dad, I'd like you to meet my friend, Cam St. Angelo."

"Nice to meet you, Mr. and Mrs. Fortner," Cam said as she turned to face them. Cam's smile fell as they surveyed her worn jeans and flannel shirt.

"Likewise," Tab's father said. "Welcome to Monroe."

"Thank you, sir."

"What's that?" Mrs. Fortner said, pointing at the wooden tiger beside Tab.

"Cam carved Mike the Tiger for me out of some cypress wood from her home. Isn't he beautiful?"

"Indeed," her mother answered crisply.

"May I see it?" her father asked with a smile.

Tab handed the tiger to him and he inspected it closely. "This is beautiful work. How long did it take?"

"Almost two months," she answered.

"Remarkable," he replied as he continued to inspect the craftsmanship. "I tried my hand at wood carving once. I damn near took my thumb off in the process. This is a beautiful piece."

"We've changed our plans and are leaving for New Orleans tomorrow," her mother said, then spun on her heel and left the room.

Tab's father looked at his daughter and handed the carving back to her with a shrug.

"What's up with her?"

"Your mom has had a burr up her butt all morning. Sorry for our early departure, but at least you'll have the run of the house." He winked.

"No problem, Dad. We may head back to campus early then to get some workouts in."

"I wish you'd stay and try to have some fun."

"We'll see, Dad." Cam could hear the disappointment in her voice.

147

"I'm cooking steaks and grilled vegetables tonight. Will you two join me while I cook and have a few beers with me while your mother stews a bit?"

"Absolutely, Dad," Tab said and stood to hug him.

"I hope you'll feel at home here, Cam. Tab speaks very fondly of you."

"I will, sir. Thank you for sharing your home with me."

"My pleasure. I'll start the grill at five, so I'll see you then."

He walked to the door and pull it closed behind him.

"That wasn't the warm reception I was hoping for. I'm sorry for Mother's attitude."

"No worries. Your dad seems pretty cool."

"He is. Sometimes I feel sorry for him for having to put up with her shit. Do you want to stay here a day or two and then go back to share New Year's with Ruth and Liz?"

"That sounds like fun to me."

†

Cam survived dinner unscathed, although Tab's mother did little to hide her disdain for the poor girl from the country who had invaded her private domain. After dinner, they excused themselves and went upstairs to watch a movie. When it ended, Tab turned to Cam. "I'm sorry, but you have to stay in the guest room next door while Mom is in the house."

Cam let out a soft laugh. "I guess I should be grateful she's not sending me to the slave quarters."

"Don't be silly, those have been converted to the spa room. Tomorrow you can move into my room, once Her Highness has left."

"Is she always this frosty?"

"Yeah, pretty much. She keeps hoping I'll bring a nice frat boy home that is worthy of her social status. For years, she's been trying to hook me up with James Buford, one of their partner's sons, but he's such a womanizer. No way I'd fall for that, even to appease my mother."

Cam could hear the sadness in Tab's voice. "I'm sorry. I should be thankful for your dad's hospitality."

Tab smiled. "He's the only reason I bother coming home. He's a great dad. By the way, he said to sleep in, that they would leave early in the morning."

"I'll stay in bed until you tell me the coast is clear."

"Okay, Cam. I'm really happy you're here."

"Me too. I loved meeting your dad."

"See you in the morning." Tab kissed her and slipped out the door.

✝

They spent the next day lazing around the house, and spent a glorious afternoon in the hot tub that was located in the spa in the old slave quarters. Tab called out for pizza, and they put a dent in her father's beer stash.

"You know, I had an interesting conversation with Wanda a few nights ago."

"What's up with her?" Tab took a sip of beer.

"She thinks she's a lesbian and came to me for girl advice. I really wish you could have been there. She's aware of our relationship and wanted to talk through some feelings."

"I'm sure you handled the situation just fine."

"It's so hard seeing them grow up. I want them to be my little sisters forever."

"No matter what age they are, they will always be your little sisters. I'm jealous that you have them in your life."

149

"They are still in the first stage of attraction, but the feelings she describes are the same ones I feel about you."

Tab reached for her hand. "That is so sweet. What advice did you give her?"

"To slow down and let fate take its course. The girl is new to the school and a year older than Wanda."

"So, she goes for the older women too, huh, just like her big sister?"

Cam chuckled. "I hadn't thought about it, but yeah, maybe she's more like me than I thought."

"It really doesn't surprise me, though. Your family is full of strong, independent females. I could easily see Sandy following your path as well."

"Yeah, she's crushing over you big-time."

"Like her big sister?"

"No, silly, I love you. This is no mere schoolgirl crush."

"I do love the sound of that. Are you about ready to head up to bed?"

"Yes, but I have one thing more I need to tell you."

"What is it, love?"

"I kind of committed us to a sleepover out on the Island this summer with Wanda and Logan. I hope you don't mind."

"That sounds like fun. Count me in."

"Thanks." Cam took her hand and led Tab upstairs.

"Ah, finally I can have you naked next to me," Tab purred when they entered her room.

They made love for hours in the luxury of Tab's king-sized bed. Cam had her howling in pleasure as her tongue and fingers expertly brought Tab to orgasm deep into the night. After a leisurely shower the next morning, they packed their bags and drove back to school.

✝

Ruth and Liz welcomed their early return, and they spent hours batting and working out. On New Year's Eve, they cooked, then sat on the apartment balcony watching the fireworks show, courtesy of the city of Baton Rouge. At midnight, Cam took Tab in her arms and kissed her.

"Happy New Year. I hope this is the first of many we will share."

"Me too," Tab answered and kissed her passionately.

"Hey, get a room, you two," Liz told them when they broke the kiss.

"Great idea." Tab took Cam's hand. "See y'all later."

†

The fireworks continued late into the night, but they were nothing compared to the heated passion between Tab and Cam. Tab pulled her into the bed and took her time teasing every part of Cam with her fingertips and a light grazing of fingernails. She loved the way Cam's skin broke out in chill bumps in the wake of her touch. The symphony of Cam's moans filled her ears as her eyes memorized every delicious curve of Cam's body. It took great restraint to keep from ravishing her lover, but Tab wanted this night to slow down to become a memory for them as they shared their first New Year's together. Her disappointment at her mother's cool reception of Cam quickly faded in the heat of her passion. Her mother be damned, Cam was the one she loved, and hoped to build a future with.

When Cam begged for Tab to bring her the sweet release of orgasm. Tab kissed her way down Cam's belly as she slipped her fingers deeply into her lover.

"Come for me, Cam," she whispered across Cam's heated skin, and when her mouth covered her swollen clitoris, Cam's body exploded. The intensity of her pleasure took Tab over the edge with her, and they molded with convulsions of pure bliss.

"I wish this night would never end," Tab told her as she lay panting.

Cam turned to face her and snuggled into Tab. "This is our beginning," she whispered and entwined her legs with Tab's.

CHAPTER ELEVEN

When the season finally arrived, Cam was excited that their first games were at home. She looked up nervously into the stands until she saw her family and waved to Sandy. She was disappointed with her first at bat, when she popped up to the shortstop. She mentally cursed herself as she bent to pick up her bat. Coach called for a time-out and walked over to Cam from the third-base coaching box.

She placed a hand on her shoulder and locked eyes with her. "Ease up on yourself. You're trying too hard. Relax, and let the real Cam come out at the plate."

"Will do, Coach." She smiled and trotted back into the dugout.

When she was on deck for her next at bat, she looked up to see Sandy watching her and shot her a thumbs-up sign. Tab had belted a base hit and there were two runners on base. Cam approached the plate, pulled the whale's tail from her jersey and kissed it while sending up a silent prayer for a hit. She tucked it back inside her jersey, tapped the packed clay from her cleats, and stepped into the batter's box. The stadium lights glowed and the crowd had fallen silent. Cam could hear her heart beating as the first pitch went wide.

I got this. I was born to play on this diamond. Cam smiled at the pitcher, and when a fastball barreled toward her, Cam's smile grew, and when the ball was met by the bat's sweet spot, she knew it was gone. Cam had belted the first home run she would hit that year. She circled the bases and got a high five from her coach.

"That's what I'm talking about," Coach said. "Great job, Cam."

When she stepped onto home plate and turned toward the dugout, the team swarmed her with congratulations. She returned to the dugout and one of the ball girls approached her and handed her a ball. "What's this?"

"Your home-run ball," the young girl told her, and smiled.

"Thanks," Cam said and took it.

"It's a tradition, and this one is very special since it's your first here," Tab explained. "Here." She handed her a pen. "Sign it and date it. After the game, add the final score and you have your first souvenir of your LSU career."

Cam did as instructed, and tucked the ball in her bag. After the game, she added the score, 6–1 and smiled, as she knew what she would do with the ball. Once the celebratory handshakes were completed postgame, Cam looked up to see Sandy rushing toward her.

"Great game," she said as she hugged Cam's neck.

"Thanks." She smiled up at the rest of her family as they approached.

"Nice game, honey," her dad said. "Do you mind Sandy staying over for tomorrow's game and we'll take her back after the game Sunday?"

"That's perfect," she answered.

154

"Congrats on your first home run and win as a Tiger. We're very proud of you."

"Thanks, Dad. I'm glad y'all were able to come."

"We'll make as many of your games as we can. You may get stuck with Squirt more often than intended, though," he teased his youngest daughter.

"She's no problem, Dad. We love having her here."

"We're going to hit the road then, so it's not too late before we get in. See you Sunday."

"Thanks again, and be safe, Dad. Love y'all."

"Love you too. Give 'em hell tomorrow."

"I will." She watched them walk away and turned to find Sandy talking with Tab.

"We're hungry," Tab informed her. "You up for some chicken fingers?"

"Heck yeah, how about you, Squirt?"

Sandy grinned. "I can always eat."

†

"Are you kidding me?" Sandy screamed.

"Nope, I want you to keep this for me," Cam said as she handed Sandy her first home-run ball.

Tab walked over to her closet and pulled down a Plexiglass-and-wood ball holder. "Here, you can place it in here."

"Thanks, Tab." Sandy took the box and accepted her assistance to place the ball inside the cube.

Cam looked at Tab. "You just had one on hand?"

"No, silly. I knew you'd be hitting a homer this weekend, so I bought it earlier."

Sandy hugged her. "Thanks, Tab."

"You do think of everything." Cam smiled at Tab.

"I try."

†

Valentine's Day fell on a Thursday, so it wasn't a problem for Cam to go home for Rudy and Bren's wedding. Tab was pleased when Cam invited her, so they planned to skip their Friday classes, then spend the night with Cam's family before driving back for a Friday night game. Sandy was thrilled to get to spend another weekend on campus. T had stepped in to serve as Bren's maid of honor, and Cam had to admit T looked much better in a dress than she would have.

When they hit town, Cam directed Tab to Bren's family home. She wanted to see her best friend for a few minutes before the day got totally crazy with wedding preparations. She also wanted to introduce her to Tab away from the crowd. When they pulled up in the yard, Suzy, one of Bren's sisters, ran inside the house to let Bren know she was there.

Bren emerged from the house and the sun hit her strawberry-blonde hair, making it glow. "I am so glad you could make it. I was worried about it being during the week."

"It just gave us a good excuse to cut classes." Cam grinned. "Bren, I'd like you to meet my partner, Tab Fortner."

Bren offered her hand, then pulled Tab into a hug and grinned when she let her go. "Like girlfriend-type partner?"

"Yes, she's my girlfriend."

Bren smiled sweetly at Tab. "You're a lucky girl. Cam's the best you'll ever find."

"Thanks, I agree with you, one hundred percent. I've heard an awful lot of good things about you."

Bren put her arm around Cam. "We've had some good times together, haven't we?"

156

"Yes, we have. It's amazing we didn't get into more trouble, though, with some of the stunts we pulled."

"She's told me about a few of them," Tab said. "Y'all were brazen young ladies."

"Our coach used to call us pure heathens," Bren admitted. "Do you have time to come in and see my dress? Mama will be pissed if you don't come in and say hello too."

"Sure," Cam said and followed her back inside. "Hey, Mama," she said when she bent down to kiss the tiny woman on the cheek. "This is my friend Tab from college. You all set to marry Bren off today?"

"Welcome, Tab. Lord, I hope we're ready. I'm sure there's some detail we've missed, but we have bride and groom, rings and wedding cake, so at least that part is taken care of."

"Everything will be beautiful, I'm sure."

"Is she going to show you the dress?"

"Yes, ma'am. I can't wait to see her in it tonight. I know she'll be beautiful."

"Y'all run along, then. I've still got food to prepare. See you tonight. Nice to meet you, Tab."

Tab smiled. "You too, ma'am."

Bren grabbed Cam by the hand and pulled her into a bedroom. A beautiful white wedding gown hung above her closet door. "That is beautiful. You can still wear white too?"

"Yes, silly. I told you I was making Rudy wait."

"That poor boy will probably explode tonight. Where are you going for your honeymoon?"

"We're driving to New Orleans tonight and he's booked us a cruise to Mexico in two days."

"Hopefully you'll be able to walk again by then," Cam teased.

†

157

Bren was as beautiful as Cam had described and Tab enjoyed watching the two of them reconnect. She knew they had been friends since elementary school and Cam had crushed on Bren for years. Cam's eyes still sparkled when she talked about Bren, but seeing them together was refreshing and Tab wasn't the least bit jealous of the relationship. In a way, it was comforting to know that Cam had such a good friend when she was growing up. That was another thing Tab had longed for as a child. No one she ever felt connected to seemed to be in the same social class her mother had perceived her family to be, so a close friendship never developed for her.

Bren had easily accepted her as Cam's girlfriend, which was another big relief. Tab was proud of Cam for introducing her as her partner. She was afraid she wouldn't feel comfortable back in her small hometown, but Cam hadn't batted an eye.

She smiled at the carefree banter between the two. Tab could sense a chapter of their lives ending with the wedding, and a family in Bren's future. Tab hoped they would continue to have a relationship as they grew into adults. Cam smiled at her, and Tab could see the happiness in her eyes. She prayed she would be enough to make Cam happy.

"I guess we'd better get a move on. Mama's probably wearing out the floor wondering where we are. You're going to make a beautiful bride." Tab saw the tears in Cam's eyes as she hugged her best friend. "We'll see you at the church later tonight."

Bren looked at Tab, then back at Cam. "Would you mind if I spoke to Tab for a minute?"

Cam looked a bit shocked, but said, "Okay, I'll go say goodbye to your mama and meet you at the car."

"Thanks," she said and kissed Cam on the cheek.

When Cam left the room, Bren turned to Tab. "I know how much she loves you, and I hope you realize the precious love she is offering you."

"I do, and I love her with all my heart. I will do everything in my power to make her happy."

"Good, the last thing you want is a crazy Cajun coming after you for breaking her heart."

Tab smiled a bit nervously. "I hear your message loud and clear, but honestly, Cam's the best thing to come into my life ever, and I never want to lose that."

"That's all I needed to hear. Thanks for coming with her. I've heard so much about you, and it was nice to finally meet you. Take care of my precious friend."

"I will give it my best."

"Thank you."

They walked out together and Cam hugged Bren a final time, then joined Tab in the car. Tab pulled away slowly and looked over to find Cam looking at her.

"Well, are you going to tell me what that was all about?"

"Just the usual 'you screw over my friend and I'll feed you to Bubba Gump' speech."

"No way, did she really mention Bubba Gump?"

"No, I embellished a bit, from your stories of him, but she threatened to hunt me down if I ever broke your heart."

Cam broke out laughing. "That's my Bren. I think she knows how happy you make me."

"That's all that matters to me. If I can keep you happy, I don't have to worry about crazy Cajuns stalking me."

Cam entwined their fingers. "I do love you."

"I love you too!"

"Let's go home," Cam said, then gave Tab the directions back to her parents' house.

†

159

"Welcome home," Camille said as she wrapped Cam in a hug. "I'm so glad you two were able to come."

"I wouldn't miss it for the world. A promise is a promise; besides, Bren would have hunted me down to take revenge if I stood her up on this important day."

"I was just getting ready to make some sandwiches for lunch. Your dad should be back any time now. Have y'all eaten yet?"

"No, ma'am, but now that you mention it, I am getting hungry. How about you, Tab?"

Tab chuckled. "I was wondering if you were ever going to feed me."

Camille hugged her tight. "I think we can handle that."

"What's Dad doing this morning?"

"Making a delivery, but he should be back shortly."

Cam knew that meant Ronny was making a delivery of 'shine to a customer somewhere, so she didn't say anything else, not wanting to get into it in front of Tab.

"What kind of sandwiches are we having?" she asked her mama.

"You can have your choice of thick-sliced bologna, ham, or turkey."

"I haven't had a bologna sandwich in years." Tab grinned. "I could go for one or two of those."

Cam smiled at her lover. "Have a seat at the table and I'll whip some up. Are mayonnaise and tomato okay for you?"

"Sounds perfect to me," Tab answered.

"How about you, Mama, what may I fix for you?"

"I can fix my own, honey."

"I know you can, but I want to do it so you can relax for a minute."

"I won't argue with that. Turkey with a slice of swiss cheese and mustard, then, please, ma'am."

"You got it. One or two?"

Camille sat at the table with a sigh. "Just one for me honey."

"Will Dad want bologna and American cheese with mayonnaise?"

"Yes, two for him, please. He's lost a bit of weight working so hard lately."

Cam frowned. "Is everything okay, Mama?"

"Oh yes. I'm sorry to worry you. T has been pulled away to help with Bren's wedding, so he's been a little shorthanded. Everything will be back to normal after tonight. Did you drop by to see Bren?"

"Yes, we did. She seems happy, and excited to be getting married."

"They'll make a great family," Camille said.

A motor hummed outside. "Sounds like Dad is arriving just in time for lunch. Tab can you pour us all some tea while I finish the sandwiches?"

"Sure, just point me to the glasses."

"Just to the right of the sink."

"Well hello there," Ronny called out as he entered the kitchen. "I'm glad to see you two have come home today."

"Thanks, Dad. Wash up and have a seat with Mama. I'll have sandwiches ready in just a minute."

He stopped to give Cam a kiss on the cheek. "Great, I'm starved." He washed his hands, then dried them and kissed Tab on the cheek as well. "Here, let me carry a couple of those," he said and picked up two glasses.

Tab carried the other two glasses to the table and returned to help Cam with the plates of sandwiches. Cam grabbed a bag of potato chips out of the pantry and brought it to the table as well. She smiled when Tab poured some chips on her plate, then opened her sandwich and placed several inside before pressing the top slice of bread down to crush them.

Cam shared a look and a grin with her mama. "Are you sure you didn't have another girl before me?"

Camille chuckled as Tab looked up to find everyone smiling at her. "No, I believe I'd remember that, but Tab sure fits in with this family."

Tab gave Cam a confused look. "Did I do something wrong?"

Cam smiled. "Nope, we all just think it's funny you put chips on your sandwich like we do."

"Oh, I love them that way." She grinned.

"We do too, so eat up," Ronny said.

Camille said to Cam, "T has moved back in with her sisters for tonight. We figured the two of you would spend the night."

"We will, but we have to get back to campus by lunchtime. We've got a ballgame tomorrow night. Do you think it would be okay if Sandy missed school tomorrow and joined us?"

"Hah. Just try getting away from here without her," Ronny teased. "We can come watch the Sunday game and bring her home, if that's good for y'all."

Tab smiled. She had grown fond of Sandy as well. "That would be perfect."

"You've got Georgia in this weekend, right?" Camille asked.

"Yes'm, we gonna have Bulldog BBQ over the weekend," Tab teased.

✝

When the girls returned from school, the house became a flurry of activity as the family prepared to attend the wedding. Ronny passed Tab in the hall, grumbling about having to wear a tie.

"Let me help you," Tab said. "I used to have to help my dad until he finally learned how to do it himself."

"Thanks." Ronny grinned at her, and within seconds, she had his knot tied.

"I'll leave it loose until you get to the church."

"I appreciate that, Tab. I feel like I'm wearing a noose."

"I can imagine. See you in a bit."

She stepped into Cam's old bedroom and her eyes widened when she saw Cam standing in front of the mirror, dressed in black dress slacks and a white tuxedo shirt, looking delicious. "You look good enough to eat," she whispered as she slipped her arms around Cam's waist.

"I'll remind you of that later tonight," Cam said as she turned in Tab's arms and kissed her.

"You won't have to remind me after I've looked at you for hours. However, my love, I think you're a bit too, um… vocal for us to make love here."

"Good point, so you'll have to wait until Sunday."

"It will be torture, but you're definitely worth the wait."

"Thanks. I'm going to check on the girls while you hit the shower."

†

The wedding was beautiful, and Tab saw a tear slide down Cam's face as Rudy kissed Bren at the end of the ceremony. Bren was gorgeous in her wedding gown, and Rudy looked just as uncomfortable in his suit as Ronny. Tab glanced over to see him tug at the tie and smiled. When they stood to honor the married couple as they departed the church, she slipped her hand in Cam's for a quick squeeze.

When they arrived at the reception, Sandy pulled them over to the food table for something to eat.

"Are you hungry?" Tab asked her.

163

Sandy grinned. "Is the Pope Catholic?"

"I know where you learned that," Tab said, and nodded toward Cam as Tab plucked a deviled egg from the tray and added it to her plate.

"Hey, go easy on those eggs. We're sharing a bed tonight," Cam teased her, and Sandy broke out in a fit of giggles. "What, do you think I'm kidding?"

"No, you're just silly, Cam."

"Yeah, maybe, but you love me."

"Tru dat," Sandy replied.

†

Cam was happy the reception wasn't a drawn-out affair. The couple opted to save the gifts for after the honeymoon, and after a quick change, the newlyweds prepared to start their new life together. Bren stopped to hug Cam and Tab before they left the reception hall, followed by the other guests.

Rudy's groomsmen had decorated his truck with the words *Just Married* and tied empty beer cans and a stuffed gator to the bumper of his truck. The crowd cheered as the bride and groom left the hall and Rudy rushed her to the truck and helped her inside. He blew the horn and they both waved to their family and friends as they raced away.

†

The team went on a streak and won fifteen games before they suffered their first loss to Bama. It was a fun-packed weekend and they did manage to take the series, winning the last two games. The final game on Sunday they informally named the Mud Bowl. A torrential rain began during the game, but there was no sign of lightning close, so they kept playing through the end of the game. The infield became soaked quickly, making sliding into a bag a soft, but a messy ordeal. Tab had made a headfirst slide into second and came up ten pounds heavier covered in mud. A terrific defensive play by Cam ended the game when she dove for a line drive at the edge of the outfield and her momentum sent her hydroplaning twenty feet into center field. They were fortunate it was the final out, because Cam swore there was no way she could have gotten to her feet to throw out a runner.

Afterward, they were all glad to reach the locker room to shower off the mud they had collected during the game. Everyone, that is, except for the team manager responsible for laundering the uniforms. Cam handed her the mud-soaked jersey, and the young woman sighed.

"I just don't know how I'm ever gonna get these things clean again."

"You'll work your magic like you always do, Carrie," Tab said as she added her jersey to the growing pile.

†

The routine of kissing the whale's tail charm before every at-bat had become part of Cam's mojo, and her success with a bat continued. Her stats brought her quickly up the ranks, not only in the SEC, but nationally. The talk around the league was that Cam was in the running for Freshman of the Year honors, and her status brought the team more television coverage of their games. Everyone on the team was happy to get more televised exposure, but Bugsy. Her obsession with Cam continued to fester even after Cam had made it clear to her that she and Tab were a couple.

The tension between them continued to escalate until one Friday night when they had a weekend off. Cam and Tab were watching movies with Liz and Ruth, and Cam decided she needed to return to the apartment to get some popcorn. She met Bugsy coming down the hallway. Bugsy had obviously been drinking.

"Well if it ain't Wonder Woman," she sneered as Cam exited the apartment.

"What's up, Bugsy?"

"I've just been out having a little fun tonight. You wanna come back to my room with me for some real fun?" Bugsy slurred, and Cam could smell the alcohol on her breath.

"I think you need to go sleep it off, Bugsy. You know we're not allowed to drink during the season."

"But I don't want to sleep it off. I just wanna have some fun with you." Bugsy grabbed for the front of Cam's shirt, and as she stumbled, she broke the chain holding Cam's charm. "What's this?" Bugsy cried out. "I've got Wonder Woman's magic charm!"

"Give it back, Bugsy," Cam requested in an angry voice.

"Are you afraid you won't be able to hit without it?" Bugsy challenged.

"I was hitting your pitches long before I ever met Tab, and she gave me the charm as a Christmas present. I don't want to hurt you, Bugsy, so please just give it back."

"You think I'm scared of you?"

Bugsy was slurring badly and swaying on her feet. Cam knew one hit would put her on the ground, but she didn't want to take advantage of Bugsy's debilitated state. She took a step back and repeated her request.

†

"What the hell is all that commotion?" Ruth asked as she looked at Liz as loud voices came from the hallway.

The three of them hurried to the door, and Ruth was the first one through just as Bugsy lunged at Cam. She rushed forward, but was too late to prevent her from grabbing Cam. "What the hell are you doing, Bugsy?"

Bugsy twirled around and looked at Ruth, Liz and Tab right behind her. "Uh-oh, the cavalry has arrived to save the day."

Tab rushed to Cam's side and looked at her torn shirt. "Are you okay?"

Cam nodded. "Yes, but she's got my charm."

Ruth saw the fury in Tab's eyes and quickly stepped between Tab and Bugsy. "Give it here, Bugsy," she demanded.

"I didn't mean nothing bad. I just wanted to have a little fun was all," Bugsy groaned. "I'm sorry, Cam," she said as she gave Ruth the charm and broken chain.

"You need to go to your apartment," Ruth growled. "I'll have to report your drinking to Coach, so don't make this any worse than it is, Bugsy."

"You're going to turn me in for drinking? Aw, c'mon, Ruth," she pleaded. "Gimme a break."

"You know the rules. It's my job. Now go, before you make things any worse for yourself."

Bugsy turned and stumbled down the hallway to the elevator and Ruth handed Cam her charm.

Tab wrapped her arms around Cam protectively and took the charm from Cam. "The chain is snapped, but I'll take care of that tomorrow. Are you okay?"

"Yes, I'm fine. I just don't understand what got into Bugsy. I've never seen her like that." She turned to Ruth. "I'm okay, so do you really have to report her?"

"Yes, Cam, I do. She broke team rules by drinking, and her behavior toward you makes it even worse. We don't treat our family like that."

Cam frowned. "What will happen to her?"

"That's entirely up to Coach. She decides all disciplinary actions but I can't turn my back on this, Cam."

"She's right, honey. If Bugsy can get away with it without repercussions, then we have no discipline. You didn't cause this, so don't feel bad."

Cam was on the verge of tears.

Tab looked at their friends. "I think we'll call it a night, ladies."

"We'll meet y'all for breakfast in the morning," Liz said and took Ruth back to their apartment.

†

Tab closed the door behind them and held a shaking Cam in her arms. "Everything's okay, baby," she whispered and kissed the top of Cam's head. "Let's climb into bed and relax."

Cam sat on the bed, still looking stunned. She allowed Tab to undress her, then curled up in her arms, still shaking. Tab stroked her back to soothe her and was relieved when Cam's trembling subsided. "I love you, Cam," she whispered.

"I love you too, Tab. I'm sorry I got so upset."

"It's not your fault. Relax and try to put this behind you."

Tab held her until Cam drifted to sleep. She wanted to go knock some sense into Bugsy, but she didn't want the situation to worsen.

†

At breakfast the next morning, Cam looked at Ruth. "Do you have to tell Coach the whole story?"

Ruth frowned. "Yes, I'm afraid I do. It's bad enough she was trashed, but attacking a teammate is uncalled for."

"Has anyone seen Bugsy this morning?" Tab asked.

Ruth nodded. "I went up to check on her earlier. As you would imagine, she's terribly hungover and sorry for attacking you, Cam."

"What do you think will happen?" Cam asked her.

"Other than a really harsh ass-chewing, I'd say a suspension from the team for a couple of weeks at least. Hopefully Coach won't boot her."

Cam's eyes flew wide. "Do you think she'd really do that?"

"For a violation of team rules, yes, she could."

"I'd really hate that for Bugsy."

Ruth smiled. "I'll do my best to talk her out of it, okay?"

"Thanks, Ruth."

"Come on, my love, we have shopping to do," Tab said as she stood from the table.

"We do?" Cam replied.

"Yes, we do. Let's go get a new chain for your charm. We've gotta keep that mojo working for you." She grinned.

"You don't think a jeweler can repair it?"

"Maybe, but I would feel better if you had a new one." She turned to Ruth and Liz. "Are you two up for dinner out on the town tonight?"

"Sounds good, what time and where?" Liz asked.

"Six o'clock, and my treat, so we gotta pick someplace good. Don's maybe for some seafood?"

Ruth smiled at Tab. "I can always eat seafood."

"See you gals later, then."

Tab and Cam returned to the apartment to get her charm before heading to town to see a local jeweler.

†

169

"Do you want me to go with you to meet Coach?" Liz asked.

"Thanks, but this is something I need to do alone. Maybe if it's just the two of us, I can convince her to go easy on Bugsy."

"I don't envy you having to meet with her. I can almost hear her fuming now."

Ruth cringed at the thought. "Yeah, me too. We'd better go if I'm going to meet her at nine."

Ruth kissed Liz and walked out to her truck to drive to Coach's office. She was surprised to see Bugsy leaning against the side.

"Do I need to go with you? I reckon you're off to meet with Coach."

"No, Bugsy. It's probably best you don't today. She'll need some time to cool down before she sees you, but expect to be called into her office tomorrow."

"Do I need to pack my bags?"

"I sure hope not, but that isn't my decision. What you did was just plain stupid, Bugsy, but we all make mistakes."

Bugsy hung her head. "Cam must really hate me now."

"Cam doesn't hate you, and she begged me not to tell Coach the whole story, but I've got no choice. This is the role Coach expects me to play, and I won't let her down. I promise you I'll do my best."

"Thanks, Ruth. I truly am sorry for my behavior."

Ruth climbed inside her truck and watched Bugsy walk back inside the building, her head hung in shame. She seemed genuinely remorseful, but Ruth wasn't sure how her behavior would fly with Coach. "Time to find out," she said and put the truck in reverse.

†

"She did what?" Coach erupted behind her desk.

"For some reason, Bugsy went out and got drunk last night. I'm not sure of the circumstances, but she let the alcohol get the better of her." Ruth cringed at the look on Coach's face. "When she met Cam in the hallway, the alcohol gave her liquid courage, or in her case liquid stupidity, to think she could make a pass."

"Is Cam okay?"

"Yes, Cam is fine, and no, before you ask, Tab did not pound Bugsy into pulp, even though she surely wanted too."

"Well, that's a relief."

"Cam asked me if I had to give you all the details, and I told her it was my job as captain. You know how compassionate she is, right?"

"Yes, I do, but that's no excuse for Bugsy's behavior. It's bad enough she broke team rules by drinking, but to attack a teammate is ludicrous."

"I agree she broke team rules, but she's young and made a stupid mistake. I truly think she's remorseful and regrets her actions. To be honest, Coach, I feel a bit sorry for her. She's a small-town kid who wants to fit in to a big world, and sometimes she just tries too hard."

Ruth was relieved to see Coach's face soften. "She's really not a bad kid. Just needs a good ass-kicking."

"So, as the captain of the team, what disciplinary action do you recommend?"

Ruth knew she would ask this question and had searched her heart for an answer. She cleared her throat. "We're not quite halfway through the season. I'd recommend a month's suspension from dressing out for games, and no travel for her."

Coach pondered. "She'd practice every day?"

"I'd suggest she be assigned to throw batting practice instead. That way she keeps her arm in shape."

"Parker could step into the pitching rotation for a month. She's been itching to start a series anyhow," Coach replied. "What else?"

Ruth smiled. "I have a new idea for you."

"Lay it on me."

"I think we need to start a fifty-mile club."

"Which is what?"

"Anyone breaking team rules has to put in fifty miles of running during the time of their suspension. It would be a deterrent for breaking the rules. It would also give them a chance to prove their motivation for returning to the team, if they dedicate themselves to knocking out the miles prior to the end of their suspension."

"How would we monitor completion?"

"I think if you asked the coach of the track team to monitor miles run for you in her team's morning workout sessions, she'd be glad to do that. They run five days a week already."

Coach's frown turned into a grin. "I do like the way you think. Two to three miles a day would give her time to think about breaking rules."

Ruth smiled. "My point exactly, Coach."

"I'm still going to call her in tomorrow for a royal ass-chewing. Before practice Monday, I'll meet with the team to discuss her suspension and the repercussions of her actions. That should minimize the gossip and hopefully curtail any further misbehavior from anyone."

"Does Bugsy need to be there for that?"

"It may be humiliating for her, but she needs to own up to her behavior. It'll be harsh, but effective. She's got a lot of talent and I would hate to see her waste this opportunity."

"I hope you'll discuss that with her tomorrow. She is talented, and her behavior could easily warrant her dismissal from the team. I'd hate to see that happen to anyone."

Coach locked eyes with her. "You can be assured that will be discussed tomorrow in great detail."

"Thanks, Coach."

"Thank you for being a great captain. Now go have some fun with that girl of yours and enjoy the rest of the weekend."

"See you Monday, Coach."

"Will you please tell Bugsy to be here at nine tomorrow morning?"

"I will and won't speak a word of our conversation to let her stew a bit longer."

"You're so wicked, but I like it. Now get out of here," Coach teased.

†

Cam and Tab were returning from their shopping adventure when Ruth pulled in beside them. They followed her into the apartment to grill her on the meeting with Coach, but even Liz was unable to coax information from her.

"I promised Coach I wouldn't tell anyone anything. Damn, that reminds me I've got to go tell Bugsy to meet her tomorrow. Be right back."

Tab looked at Liz, who just shrugged as Ruth left the apartment. "You know how she is. If asked not to tell, she won't spill a word."

"I just hope it didn't go too badly for Bugsy," Cam replied.

"Coach would be meeting with her today if she was giving her the boot," Tab said.

"You think so?" Liz asked.

"Yeah, I think she's being a coach and letting Bugsy worry another day before she meets with her."

Cam placed her palms together and looked toward the ceiling. "Dear Lord, please keep me from ever making Coach mad." Liz and Tab broke out in laughter. "Hey, I'm serious. I never want to get on that woman's bad side."

Tab smiled. "I agree completely with you, darling."

Ruth walked back in smiling. "What, you don't have the TV on yet? Don't ya know Bama's playing the Tennessee Vols today?"

Liz groaned. "Damn, I did forget. I'll order some pizza while you get the game on. The usual, ladies?"

"Sounds good to me," Cam answered and snuggled in next to Tab on the couch.

†

Bugsy's stomach churned with anxiety as she walked to Coach's office the next morning. Her hangover didn't help, and she rushed into the hedges outside the fieldhouse to purge the acid from her stomach. When the dry heaves ended, she walked into the restroom inside the field house to rinse her mouth and bathe her heated face in the cool water. She ripped off a paper towel to dab her face, and when she saw her reflection in the mirror, she cringed. Her eyes were red and swollen. She looked like she'd been up for days.

"Stupid, stupid, stupid," she growled at her reflection. With nothing left to purge, she tossed the paper towel into the trash. "Time to face the music." She exited the restroom and walked to Coach's office. Her hand trembled as she knocked on the door.

†

"Come in," Coach called out. She glared at Bugsy as the young athlete shuffled into her office. "Take a seat. You need to do some explaining about your behavior, and it damned well better be good." Bugsy trembled after she took a seat, and Coach walked around to lean back on her desk. "Just what the hell were you thinking? Not only did you violate team rules by drinking during the season, you also assaulted a teammate. I don't know which poor decision is the worst offense." Bugsy hung her head. "What do you have to say on your behalf?"

"That I'm probably the stupidest player you've ever had. I made two tragic mistakes that I wish I could take back, but I can't justify my behavior. I'm sorry for disappointing you and the team, Coach."

Bugsy looked up and cringed as Coach leaned toward her. "There is no justification for what you did, and I was tempted to send you packing, if for no other reason than to make an example of your poor decision making to the rest of the team."

"I deserve that, Coach, but if you'll give me another chance, I promise it will never happen again."

"Damn straight it won't. You should be grateful Ruth is your team captain. I was ready to suspend you from the team indefinitely when she came to me, but she convinced me to try something different with you. Apparently, she sees the same talent in you that I did and came up with an alternative." Coach sat on the edge of the desk. "Starting today, you're on a month-long suspension. You will continue to practice with the team, but you will not dress out for games or travel to away games. You will throw batting practice every day to keep your arm in shape. You will also run with the track team every weekday morning. You will run fifty miles during the time of your suspension, which should give you plenty of time to contemplate your

175

behavior." She stood and walked around the desk to sit in her chair. "The track coach will record your miles and update me weekly. If you fail to log in the mileage, don't bother to give me excuses, just pack your bags. Do you understand?"

"Yes, Coach, I do, and I promise I'll do everything you ask."

"There won't be any other second chances. Is that clear?"

"Yes, Coach. Thank you."

"Be at the track at five tomorrow morning. I'll see you at practice tomorrow afternoon."

Bugsy nearly jumped out of the chair and walked to the door.

"Bugsy," she called.

Bugsy turned back to face her. "Yes, Coach?"

"I can't tell you to never drink again, but if it's an issue for you, get it under control before it ruins your life."

"It won't, Coach. I made a stupid decision. It won't happen again."

"Good. Now get out of here. I've got work to do."

"Yes, Coach."

CHAPTER TWELVE

When the regular season ended, they had lost only seven games and were in third place in the SEC standings going into the conference tournament in Oxford, Mississippi. After a first-round victory, they dropped game two to the conference-leading Gators and were forced to fight their way back through the loser's bracket. They faced Bama in the semifinals and lost by one run. Coach pulled them together after the game.

"You played a great game and lost to a good team, so hold your heads high. Your hard work and success over the season is good enough to move us into the regionals."

Cam breathed a sigh of relief and cheered with the rest of her team.

"Texas, here we come," Tab said and high-fived her.

Coach calmed the group by waving to gain the players' attention. "We have time to return to the hotel for showers then come back for the final, or we can clean up and go eat."

"I think it's a probability that we'll play one or both of these teams again in the tournament," Tab said. "I think we need to watch the game."

Coach smiled. "Great choice, Tab. Let's go get cleaned up and come back for the game. Then we're going for the biggest steaks we can find."

✝

The team quickly forgot losing at the conference tournament when they got to Austin and easily won the regional to move on to the super regional in Michigan. They won the first game of the series and lost the second. More devastating than the loss was the injury Tab sustained sliding into third. She went into a headfirst slide and her left wrist jammed under the bag, snapping her forearm three inches above the wrist. Cam's concentration was lost as she watched the paramedics place an inflatable splint on her arm. Tab was in obvious pain as they stabilized her wrist, and Cam's heart ached for her lover. Tab refused to go to the hospital until after the game ended, staying instead to cheer for her team.

"You've got to get your head back in the game," Tab warned Cam after she booted a routine grounder for her first error of the postseason.

Cam had her emotions under control when she came up to bat in the bottom of the seventh, with two runners on and the team down by four. The first pitch she drove foul down the right field line, but out of the park. The home crowd let out a collective sigh of relief when the wind carried the ball out of bounds. Cam was back in the zone, and the next pitch she took deep to center field, for her thirty-fourth home run of the year, a new freshman record, but the team was still down by one run. Ruth followed her with a single, but the next batter hit into a double play to end the game.

Cam climbed into the back of the ambulance with Tab. "I'll get the team settled and meet you at the hospital," Coach told them.

†

X-rays confirmed the broken ulna, and Tab received a sedative prior to the painful process of setting the bone. Cam held her hand as the emergency-room physician set the bone as gently as he could and sent her for another x-ray to assure proper bone placement, before sending her off to casting.

When they entered the casting area, the tech looked at a loopy Tab and asked, "Do I need to guess what color cast you'd like?"

Tab smiled up at her. "LSU purple, of course."

"You got it," she answered. "Did you win?" she asked as she began applying the plaster.

"Nope, we lost by one, but have one more chance tomorrow," Cam said.

"No more ball for me this year," Tab groaned.

Coach walked in to hear her comment. "No, but we still have another shot of making it to Oklahoma City. How are you feeling?"

"I'm not feeling anything right now, Coach," Tab slurred, still under the effects of the medication.

Coach looked up at Cam. "That won't last once the sedative wears off. Did they give her some pain medicine?"

Cam held up a bag, "Already filled."

"Good, she's going to need them. I've already given them the insurance information, so as soon as she's done here, we can head back to the hotel. The team's already

179

getting ready for dinner, but I think it'll be room service for you two tonight."

"Thanks, Coach. I don't think she's going to be up to a restaurant dinner tonight."

"Okay, she may still be a little damp, so no swimming pool or hot tubbing tonight," the tech teased. She handed Cam a roll of plastic sleeves. "Make sure she uses these when she showers."

"Will do, thanks," Cam answered.

"Are you ready to roll out of here?"

Tab looked at the tech with groggy eyes. "Yes, ma'am, let's do it."

Cam focused on Tab. The sound of applause filled the air when the wheelchair brought Tab out. They looked up to see the bus and Cam smiled as their teammates continued to cheer.

"Wow, I wasn't expecting this," Coach said. "It's pretty awesome, though," she said to one of her assistant coaches.

"They wanted to come here instead of the hotel," she answered.

"That's my girls," Coach said as her team surrounded Tab with hugs and well-wishes.

†

In the top of the seventh inning with a runner on first and one out, Cam called for a time-out. Bugsy was pitching the game, and Cam called the infield together. Ruth trotted out from behind the plate. "What's up Cam?"

"We can do this. With a ground ball, we can turn a double play and end the inning. We're only down by one run." She looked at Bugsy. "Give her a low ball to force a grounder and trust your defense to turn a double play. We can do this, Tigers."

They broke the huddle and resumed their defensive positions. The batter came to the plate, and Ruth called for a curve ball, low and on the outside corner of the plate. Bugsy started her windup and released the pitch.

"Ball one," the umpire cried out.

The pitch had missed the plate by an inch.

"You can do this, Bugsy," Ruth yelled as she tossed the ball back to the pitcher's mound.

Bugsy caught the ball and turned away from the plate to pick up a resin bag. She looked at Cam.

"You got this," Cam shouted and smiled.

Bugsy returned her smile, dropped the bag, then turned back to face the batter. She peered in for the sign from Ruth.

Ruth called the same pitch. Cam watched as the ball approached and the batter started to swing. The ball struck the bat, heading toward Parker playing second base, as she broke to cover the bag. Parker tossed the ball to her in stride, and Cam released a bullet to Liz at first. It was close, but the long stretch Liz made was enough to turn the double play on the speedy runner.

"Yes!" Cam cried out and high-fived her team as they headed for the dugout. "Now let's get the bats working."

Michigan brought in their ace pitcher to finish off the inning. While she was throwing her warm-up pitches, Coach called the team together. She nodded toward the field. "She's got a wicked fastball, and she's rested, so be ready." She turned her attention to Liz. "You're up first. Be ready and jump on the first strike you see. She'll only get stronger with each pitch." Then she turned to Cam. "If Liz gets on base, you can forget getting anything close to hit. I would intentionally walk you, and I'm sure they will think hard about giving you anything close enough to hit." All eyes turned to Parker. "That puts the pressure on you for a hit."

"You can do this," Cam assured her. "Wink at her with those pretty green eyes, and knock the heck out of the ball."

Parker and the group laughed, easing the tension.

"Cam's right, you can do this. A hit is all we need to score a run and guarantee extra innings. Two runs and we'll win. Let's do this, Tigers."

"Batter up," the umpire called.

Cam walked with Liz as far as the on-deck circle. "Give 'em hell," she said as Liz walked to the plate. Cam took several practice swings as Liz settled at the plate.

The umpire saw her ready and called out, "Play ball."

Cam was on deck and fixed her eyes on the pitcher, and when she started her windup, she paced the flight of the ball with her eyes and swung her bat to gauge the speed of the pitch. The pitch was off the plate.

"Ball one," came the call.

"You got this. Come on, Liz," Cam called to her.

The catcher returned the ball to the pitcher, who threw it into her glove several times, making a loud pop, as if to settle her nerves.

The pitcher started her windup, and Liz readied her bat. She swung through the air and the crowd cried out when the pitch sailed inside and struck Liz in the upper arm as she tried to dodge it.

"Take your base, batter."

Liz dropped her bat and jogged down the first-base line, rubbing the sting from her arm.

The bat girl raced past Cam to retrieve Liz's bat as she walked to the plate.

"Time out," the Michigan coach called from the dugout, and walked out to the pitcher's mound.

Cam turned to look at Coach, who was walking down the third-base line toward her. She took several steps to meet her.

"She's probably taking the bat out of your hands, but be ready just in case."

"I'll be ready, Coach."

The Michigan coach trotted back to the dugout after speaking to her infield, and Cam approached the plate and readied herself for the pitch. She took out her charm and kissed it before tucking it back into her jersey.

"Play ball."

Cam locked her eyes on the pitcher, and inwardly groaned when she caught movement out of the corner of her eye. The catcher left her crouched position, and stepped to the right of the plate.

"Ball one."

Damn. I was hoping I'd get a chance.

As Coach had predicted, an intentional walk occurred rather than taking a chance Cam would go yard. She dropped her bat and jogged to first base, then turned and pointed to Parker. "It's on you."

Parker nodded and approached the plate.

The crowd fell silent as the first pitch arrived, dead in the center of the plate and Parker drove it deep to center field. Cam and Liz had to freeze between bags until they were sure the ball wouldn't be caught, but it sailed over the center fielder's head and ricocheted off the wall. She played the ball perfectly, hitting the shortstop with a perfect strike. Cam reached second before the ball rifled back into the infield, then turned to cringe when she realized Liz was on her way to home plate. She was a sitting duck and easily tagged out by the catcher.

"My bad, Liz," Coach called out as Liz trotted back to the dugout. "Good job, Parker." She looked at Cam and called out, "One out, Cam."

Ruth came up next and laced a line drive down the first-base line. Cam blasted off second and grinned when she saw

183

Coach signaling for her to head home. Her foot smacked the base as she rounded for home.

"Get down," she heard Tab call from the dugout and went in hard in a headfirst slide, beating the catcher's tag, and the game was tied.

"Time-out," Coach called and sent in a pinch runner for Ruth. "Great job, Ruth."

Carrie, the next batter, struck out, and Loren hit a line drive, but right to the shortstop.

The game went into extra innings to break the tie. They played two scoreless innings until Michigan plated a runner. If one of the hitters ahead of her could get on, Cam would have another at bat. The first two batters struck out, and Liz came up to bat.

"Get on base, Liz," she said as they walked out together. Liz worked the pitcher to a full count, and the next pitch was a wild pitch and she drew a walk. Cam's heart pounded as she kissed her charm and walked to the plate.

"Time-out," the Michigan coach growled, and Cam walked down to chat with Coach.

"Will they pitch to me?"

"I wouldn't." Coach grinned at her. "The first pitch will tell. If you like it, take it."

Cam smiled at the confidence Coach had in her. "You got it, Coach."

"Get 'em, Tiger," Coach said and turned back toward third.

Cam glanced into the dugout at her team. They all turned their caps backward for the rally-cap gesture and she locked eyes with Tab.

"You got this," Tab shouted.

Cam smiled at her and returned to the plate.

The first pitch was a fastball, and Cam drove it deep, but foul, down the third-base line. She watched Coach dance, trying the wave the ball back into the field of play, but it crossed left of the foul pole.

"Straighten it out, Cam," Coach encouraged her.

Cam took a deep breath and stepped back into the batter's box. She shut out the world and concentrated only on the pitch. The pitcher released another fastball, this one perfectly in her wheelhouse. Cam timed her swing and felt the impact of the ball meeting the bat. She knew it was a strong hit and raced down to first base. The crowd watched as the centerfielder tracked the flight of the ball as it approached the wall. She timed her jump perfectly and had just enough reach to capture it in her glove as it flew over the fence. Cam watched in horror, then dropped to her knees. She had failed her team.

The magic of the season was lost as the game ended and the team lost by a run.

The Michigan fans roared with applause at the miraculous defensive play and Coach ran over to Cam and placed an arm around her shoulders. "That was one helluva catch. You gave it everything you had, so be as proud of yourself as I am."

Cam nodded, but couldn't hold back disappointed tears. She brushed them away and joined her team in the postgame handshakes. The Michigan coach also slipped an arm around Cam. "You played a great game, young lady. We'll see you next year. Chin up."

During the aftergame huddle, tears filled the team's eyes. After all their success during the year, there would be no trip to OKC for the Lady Tigers of LSU this season.

Coach joined them in the huddle. She took a few seconds to lock eyes with each of her players. "I couldn't be prouder of a group of fine athletes. The determination and effort y'all put into this season was exemplary. Even though we didn't reach Oklahoma City, we still have had a terrific season and have new experiences to build on. If you work as hard next year, I have no doubts we will be making that trip. Thank you one and all for making this a terrific season." She looked at Ruth and smiled. "I've got some additional news that I'd like to share with you. First, Ruth Sasser will stay on with us as a graduate assistant, and second, the university has approved us hosting two, one-week softball camps this summer. So enjoy time with your families until the middle of June and stay in shape."

Cam was happy to hear all the good news. It helped to take a bit of the sting of the loss away.

Tears of disappointment wiped away, the team returned to the hotel.

†

Cam's cell phone rang as they entered the room. Sandy was on the phone when she answered.

"Yeah, I know I got robbed. It was a great hit. ... Thanks, I'm glad you're still proud of me. ... Yes, I'll call you when we get back to town."

"You played a helluva game," Tab said when she ended the call. "I couldn't be more proud of you."

"Thanks, that really helps, but it still hurts that we fell short."

"I understand, but we'll get there."

Cam showered with Tab, and as they dried off to dress for dinner, Tab looked at her. "We're still going."

"Going where, my love?"

"To Oklahoma City, for the championship. I booked us a room and tickets to the tournament when you were on the phone with the family. The only question that remains is will you drive me?" She held up her casted arm.

186

"I'll drive you anywhere you want to go." Cam grinned and hugged her. "I love you."

"Love you too, baby."

"I've got one more final to take, and then we can go. When did you want to leave?"

Tab checked her phone. "I've got reservations starting next Wednesday, so after your final we can pack up and go."

"That sounds perfect."

†

The tournament was the largest softball event Cam had ever been to. When they walked into the stadium for the first time, her eyes widened with excitement. She had dreamed of playing on this diamond for years, and would have three more shots of making it to the championships. They had defeated every team in the championship during the regular season, which bolstered her confidence. They would make it next year.

Even though the team hadn't reached the finals, Cam and Tab's presence drew the attention of coaches and players. They both received high praise for their performance during the year, and Tab's cast had much ink added to it by the end of the tournament.

They were present for every pitch, wishing to soak up every memory to share with the team to help motivate them for next season. Tab bought T-shirts for them both, along with another to hang up in the locker room as a reminder of their ultimate goal for next season.

Tab had gotten them great seats, and before the beginning of the final game, she turned to Cam. "Next year, we will be on the opposite side of this fence. I just know it."

"I do too," Cam said. "We were so close, but we will still chase that dream."

187

ABOUT THE AUTHOR

ALI SPOONER

Ali Spooner, a native of Florida, now calls Pensacola her forever home. Ali has been writing for many years as a hobby, and with the assistance of the Affinity Rainbow Publishing, team has taken her love of storytelling to a new level.

Ali's characters range from cowgirls and psychics, to a healthy dose of supernatural beings. She has written stand-alone titles and series. Ali is an avid reader and her other hobbies include photography, outdoor activities and watching college sports.

OTHER AFFINITY BOOKS

<u>Unconventional Lovers</u> by Annette Mori

Bri and Siera are young women with huge hearts and strong wills; they want nothing more than to find a peaceful and secure space to be themselves. But the world is a harsh place for anyone who is different. Bri's Aunt Olivia is a vet who channels her emotions into her work and her love of Bri. Siera has her Aunt Deb who adores her. Despite their individual battles against hurt, prejudice and rejection, can these four women find love against the odds?

<u>Say You Won't Go</u> by JM Dragon & Erin O'Reilly

Logan Perry spent part of an inheritance traveling to various states, unconsciously looking for something to focus her life on. Taryn Donovan has no self-esteem and hates the waitressing job that barely keeps her in food. Can an unexpected weekend encounter turn out to be something more fulfilling? Find out in this sexually charged romance.

<u>Playing with Matches</u> by Lacey Schmidt

Dr Augusta Stuart has devoted her adult life to supporting the mental health of disadvantaged children and moves to a new clinic in San Antonio. Her friend sets her up on a date with Callia Alexana. Prickly debates are somehow as unexpectedly fascinating as playing with matches, and Gus is forced to consider what preconceptions she is willing to burn to find true love.

Changing Perspectives by Jen Silver
Art director, Dani Barker, lives life on the edge and finance director Camila Callaghan thinks it's necessary to stay in the closet to maintain her position. When Dani and Camila meet, they both sense an attraction, A change of perspective for both women is needed if they are to act on it.

Death is Only the Beginning by JM Dragon
What would you do if you were in a fatal accident with a stranger and ended up in heaven with them? Only to find out it wasn't an accident, it was murder. Follow the ghostly adventures of these two acrimonious strangers, who help two women find love and find closure for their predicament.

For the Love of a Woman by S. Anne Gardner
Enter a world where oil is supreme, passion rules reason and there is always the threat of civil war. In this jungle of power Raisa Andieta resides as one of its masters. Her only desire is to rule it alone. Carolyn Stenbeck is just trying to keep her marriage together. Her only desire is to be able to escape and never look back. When Raisa and Carolyn meet, it is like fuel and fire…a storm is brewing. Civil War is in the air, and passion like the coming storm begins to erupt.

The Bee Charmer by Ali Spooner
After the death of her father, Nat St. Croix needs to decide on which direction her life should take. Does she continue her life alone, as a trapper and trader, or does she start over and

try to fit into a town surrounded by strangers? Will the call of the wild and all that is familiar win out, or will the call of love capture Nat's heart?

The Organization by Annette Mori & Erin O'Reilly
The feisty, fiery women from Asset Management are back for another heart-stopping adventure! This time, their sights are set on a new mob boss Leonid Petrov. Val is tagged as the go-to member to infiltrate Leonid's inner circle. Tasked with keeping Leonid's impossible new wife, Gina, safe, Val encounters more problems than solutions. Will wild card Gina be Val's Achilles heel and lead to her demise, or will it fill her with a strength she didn't know she had?

Running From Love by Jen Silver
Sam Wade returns home from a business trip to discover her wife, Beth, has left her for another woman, Lydia. To take her mind off the breakup, Sam accepts an assignment to learn to play golf at the newly opened Temperley Cliffs Golf Resort in Cornwall not knowing that is where Beth and Lydia plan to go too. There is more than one way to run from love; from never having to make a commitment and say those magical three words, "I love you." Find out what happens when they find themselves together—sport, betrayal, jealousy, and love form an unforgettable fusion of emotions.

Affinity
Rainbow Publications

eBooks, Print, Free eBooks

Visit our website for more publications available online.

www.affinityrainbowpublications.com

Published by Affinity Rainbow Publications
A Division of Affinity eBook Press NZ LTD
Canterbury, New Zealand

Registered Company 2517228